What the critics are saying

"Definitely not to be missed." - *Michelle Gann, The Word on Romance*

"This is the second book in Marly Chance's Oath series and I highly recommend both. This was a fun read from the beginning and I couldn't put it down." - *Laura Lane for Sensual Romance*

"This highly anticipated sequel to *Oath Of Seduction* was well worth the wait." - *B Small for Paranormal Romance*

"This is a fast paced, exciting, sexy romance that is guaranteed to keep you reaching for a nice cool drink." - *Terrie Figueroa, Romance Reviews Today*

Ellora's Cave Publishing, Inc.
PO Box 787
Hudson, OII 44236-0787

ISBN # 0-9724377-2-X

Edited by Martha Punches.
Cover art by Darrell King.

Warning: The following material contains strong sexual
content meant for mature readers. *Oath of Challenge:
Conquering Kate* has been rated NC-17, erotic, by three
independent reviewers. We strongly suggest storing this
book in a place where young readers not meant to view
it are unlikely to happen upon it. That said, enjoy...

OATH OF CHALLENGE:

Conquering Kate

Written by

Marly Chance

To my husband, who is my best friend, my true romantic hero, and the best part of my life. I love you more than I can say.

To my readers and friends, who have been very encouraging and supportive about my stories. It means so much to me!

To all the dreamers out there, who struggle each day to achieve the impossible.

With my love and deepest gratitude for helping me make my own dream come true.

Thank you.

Prologue

The Shimerian population had been in trouble for many generations. There was a great disproportion of males and not enough female mates. Of the children born, a large percent were male. It was a downward spiral that spelled eventual extinction for an entire planet. Shimerian scientists worked feverishly to solve the mystery of the population problem, but were unsuccessful. As a temporary solution they proposed importing females from other planets or having males go off-planet for mates.

After listening to the scientists' grim reports, Shimerian government officials began to look for possible solutions. They studied other planets and concluded that Earth, with its many similarities, was a logical first choice.

Humans and Shimerians were similar biologically. The two planets were environmentally similar, although there were significant differences in atmosphere. However, these differences presented a major difficulty. Shimerians could not adapt well enough to the differences to live on Earth for longer than three weeks at a time. After three weeks they grew progressively sicker until death occurred.

Humans, on the other hand, were more adaptable. They were able to adjust to Shimerian atmosphere quickly and could live on the planet with no problem. Even more importantly, Shimerians and humans were biologically compatible enough to make interplanetary reproduction possible. A solution was in sight.

After lengthy negotiations, the Earth government agreed to help. The ShimEarth Friendship Treaty was signed. The Treaty was supposed to be the beginning of a new era in interplanetary cooperation for the greater good.

Earth agreed to provide potential mates for Shimerians. In return, Shimerian resources and technology were fully available to Earth. Already, in only the first eighty years since the signing, amazing cures for some of the worst Earth diseases had resulted from the cooperative knowledge provided by Shimerian scientists to Earth scientists.

However, the sharing of technology and culture was approached slowly and carefully. No one wanted conflict resulting from too rapid an integration. Each planet had its own secrets, but positive advances took place on both sides. Each government had its own reasons for ensuring success.

However, in the beginning, suspicion ran high. The Treaty was complicated to negotiate and even more difficult to implement. The Earth government, making clear it was not prostituting its women, agreed to provide a register of potential mates and carefully agreed upon Courtship Laws.

Since the Shimerian males' version of courtship leaned toward kidnapping and seduction, the Earth government had been very specific that the program would be voluntary and follow prescribed rules. Earth females chosen from the register or "called to Oath," were given three courtship or engagement options, two of which included a "knowing period."

If, after the knowing period and under certain conditions, the Earth female did not want to continue the union, she could file legal paperwork that the union was incompatible and should be dissolved. The third option was added in the event that a female had changed her mind. Basically, Earth officials tried to build in an escape clause. In the end, Shimeria was able to turn the clause to its advantage.

The register was considered by Earth to be similar to signing a contract with the armed services. Females signed and swore an oath to abide by the Oath contract. The penalties for breaking Oath were quite severe--imprisonment and heavy monetary fines. However, the social stigma of breaking Oath was considered much worse.

When the treaty had been signed some eighty years ago, there was hesitation by Earth females and only a few actually became Shimerian mates. However, as the positive breakthroughs in technology and medicine began to be widely felt, the Shimerian government pushed hard for a public relations program in higher learning centers to promote registering.

These "culture classes" explained the process in glowing terms and encouraged young women to register. The classes had a very idealistic slant with just enough excitement to entice. "*Help your fellow human beings and Shimerians, too,*" they persuaded, *"while having an adventure."*

More Earth females registered and were mated. Then, rumors began to surface about Shimerian men and their sexual abilities. Women spoke with sighs of their physical attributes, but a lot of information remained unknown. There was just enough mystery to intrigue and entice even the most hardheaded of women. More and more Earth females registered.

After a while, the overwhelming response meant that for every twenty thousand Earth women registered, only one would actually be called to Oath. Most would go on to fall in love with a man on Earth. When she married or at age thirty, her name would be removed from the register with thanks from her government for her willingness to serve.

Shimeria conducted its own educational campaign. Shimerian males were given "Earth culture classes" in school to understand the customs and the languages. In addition, more emphasis was placed on the importance of honing telepathic skills.

Shimerian males realized early that finding a mate was a difficult task. It involved years of telepathically probing and searching for their destined mate. When the male located his mate mentally, the odds were very good that she would be on the Earth register. If she was not on the register, there were other alternatives.

After all the years of practicing and searching, it was quite a moment for a Shimerian male to locate his mate. Some males went through their lifetime trying and not succeeding. No one could understand why some males located their mates at a particular time. It was a great mystery and a great source of frustration. Some called it luck. Some said chance. Some said destiny. And some said skill.

Some, like Tair da'Kamon considered it all of those things. Knowing Tair's skills, not many would dare to disagree. In the last few weeks, Tair's brother, Liken had called his mate to Oath. Rumor held that Tair had located his pactmate years ago, but had waited. Whisperers said he had been waiting for his brother to call his mate, so that Tair could be the couple's link. To be eligible to offer protection as a link, the male had to be unpledged at that time. Tair was very protective of his brother. Most felt the rumor could be entirely true.

Now that Liken was pledging with his mate and Tair was her link, many wondered if Tair would call his pactmate to Oath. Speculation was rife regarding his possible mate. He was a Guardian of exceptional skill, respected for his cunning and determination. What kind of Earth female would be a match for such a warrior?

Tair heard the new rumors and arched an eyebrow in sardonic amusement. As usual, he kept his own counsel. He never confirmed or denied anything. Gossipmongers were left to wonder. However, later in private, Tair did not bother hiding his lusty smile of anticipation. Indeed, he had found his mate. Her name was Kate...

Chapter 1

Men, Kate concluded, are pretty much like an expensive pair of stockings -- sexy when you first try them on, but apt to run like hell at the first snag. Leaning back in her chair, she sighed and waved a mental goodbye to Todd.

He had been an amusing lover and a nice diversion from the drudgery of her heavy work schedule. It was a shame that he had to disappear and take her good sex life with him. Truthfully, she rather thought she'd miss the sex more than Todd.

Suddenly, a deep masculine voice broke her train of thought. "I've heard that sigh before. It can only mean trouble."

Kate smiled with surprised pleasure. "I'm not the troublemaker in this family, remember? Gage, what are you doing here?"

Gage strolled into her office and sat down with unconscious masculine grace. Kate assessed her brother silently. He was six foot, three with blond hair and blue eyes. Muscular and athletic, he had an easy charm to match.

Under the movie star good looks, though, he looked tired. She could see traces of strain in his face, and there was a lurking sadness in those crystal blue eyes. Frowning with concern, she continued, "And why do you look so sad?"

Gage rolled his eyes, though affectionately. "Men do not get sad, Kate. Women get sad. Men get pissed off. And I'm not either of those things. I'm fine. You're the one sighing. What's the sigh all about?"

Kate stared hard at him a moment, but knew he wouldn't be budged. He wasn't going to tell her until he was ready. She didn't like seeing that look on his face at all. She could guess why it was there, and the mere thought sent a touch of panic through her veins.

Her brother would not die. She would fight fate, or God, or whomever she had to fight, but she was not losing Gage. Pasting a determined smile on her face, she said lightly, "I could be sighing at the thought of the chocolate ice cream I had at lunch."

Gage threw back his head and laughed. Shaking his head at her, he said, "First of all, you don't like ice cream. A horrible sin, but it's true. Secondly, knowing you, you probably worked right through lunch. Unless you lunched with, uhhh what's the name this time? Was it Brad or Brent?"

Kate gave him a cold glare designed to freeze the blood in his veins. "It was neither. Do try to keep up. His name was Todd. And he's outlived his usefulness as of this morning."

Gage's expression sobered a little, but the amusement was still in his voice. "Poor bastard. What did you do? Tell him he was fired without further notice? Oh, I know, you're both lawyers. You sent him papers addressed to 'Dumpee.'"

Kate forced a rather brittle laugh and nearly winced. "Actually, I believe I received the papers this time. But, no doubt he'd have received some from me soon enough."

Gage sat up and searched her face with suddenly gentle eyes. "Kate, are you okay? Did you really care about this one?"

Kate sighed and felt a pang of sadness that had nothing to do with Todd. "No, actually, I didn't. I mean, I cared about him as a person, but you know me–I don't develop lasting relationships."

Gage shook his head. "That's not true and you know it. Look at you and Sharon. You've been friends for forever. "

Kate went cold with icy dread at the mention of Sharon. Taking a deep breath, she said with resignation, "Sharon. That's right. You don't know about Sharon."

Looking really alarmed now, Gage asked, "What's happened?"

Kate met his eyes squarely. "Sharon was called to Oath. She's due back from Shimeria today. I have the incompatibility papers already drawn up for her signature. "

Gage eyes widened in shock. "Called to Oath? Sharon?" He looked dazed at the thought. "Sharon is so…"

He fell silent, obviously trying to think of a term. "And Shimerians are so…"

Kate smiled grimly. "Yes, exactly. If they've harmed her in any way, I'll go there myself and see justice done. I swear I will."

Thoughts of her sheltered librarian best friend in the arms of a dominant, sexually aggressive alien had given Kate quite a few sleepless nights in the last three weeks. Thank God Sharon was coming home today. She would see her and make sure everything was okay. Feeling a familiar sense of frustration at her inability to do anything now, she focused on explaining the specifics to Gage.

"His name is Liken da'Kamon. He invoked the Oath three weeks ago and Sharon chose Seduction." Her mind filled with images of herself and Sharon at eighteen, so young and idealistic, signing the register. Wincing at the thought of how she'd urged Sharon to sign, she felt a fresh wave of guilt and helplessness.

Gage knew he looked outwardly composed. He'd had a lifetime of hiding his emotions, even from his sister. But inside he was truly shocked and worried at the news. Straightening his shoulders, he asked precisely, "What do you mean she chose Seduction?"

Kate heard the dangerous edge to his voice and said quietly, "Earth females get three options as to the Oath the Shimerian male will make: Seduction, Challenge, or Capture."

Gage tried to remember what he could about Shimeria. It wasn't much. He had met some Shimerian males in his travels, but he'd never been off-planet to visit the place. The males whom he'd met were big and lusty types, powerfully built and aggressively male. He couldn't imagine Sharon with that kind of man.

He felt a growing anger at the thought of what might have happened to Sharon. Focusing on getting as much information as possible, he said shortly, "Explain the options to me. What exactly happens?"

Kate watched the growing anger in her brother and felt a little relieved. They would help Sharon together. Taking another deep, calming breath, she said, "I've been going over the paperwork carefully. If the female chooses Seduction, she goes to Shimeria with him for three weeks referred to as a "knowing period." He gets certain intimacies at certain times progressively."

She realized she was tapping her fingers impatiently on the desk out of sheer nerves and stopped immediately. "Total intimacy occurs within three days. Basically, he takes an oath to seduce her into staying with him. After three weeks, if he's successful, they have a pledge ceremony and go back to Shimeria to live. If he's unsuccessful in convincing her to stay at the end of the knowing period, she can file incompatible papers and dissolve the pact."

Gage tensed even more and said shortly, "Couldn't she have picked one of the other options?"

Kate sighed. "Believe me, for Sharon that would have been worse. The Oath of Challenge is similar to the Seduction Oath. The female agrees to cooperate sexually with any intimacy for two weeks--except intercourse. Obviously, he can't abuse her or force her into repulsive acts. He's challenging her to explore her sexuality without giving in to total intimacy."

The words came out huskier than she intended. Clearing her throat, she continued, "If she has intercourse with him, she is ineligible to file for noncomp. She has to pledge with him and stay."

Kate felt a little warm at the discussion of the Challenge Oath. Despite her worry for Sharon, she couldn't help feeling intrigued at the thought. What would it be like to explore your desires in that way?

An image of a Liken's broad-shouldered brother flashed through her mind. There was something about him. He kept popping into her thoughts. She had even awakened from a few rather interesting dreams. She might see him today when she went to the Pactbuilding to see Sharon and file the papers. Immediately, she banished the thought.

With each sentence, Gage could feel his blood pressure rising. "And Capture?"

Shrugging helplessly, Kate explained, "In my opinion, it's the most dangerous of the three. The female runs and tries to evade the male for a month. She has two advantages: she gets a 24-hour head-start and Shimerians can only stay on Earth for three weeks without getting ill. The illness progresses rapidly and is fatal if they don't return to their own world. They can't adjust to our atmosphere."

She wearily rubbed the back of her neck where it had begun to ache. "I wish we couldn't adjust to their atmosphere, but we can."

Gage felt guilt all the way down to his toes. He had been unavailable and out of touch when his family needed him. He felt the guilt turn to anger at his own selfishness. He should have been there for them.

He said, "I'm sorry, Kate. The two of you should have been able to come to me. I would have helped hide her. He wouldn't have found her. And if he had, he wouldn't have taken her away."

Kate smiled and shook her head. "Gage, as much as I appreciate the protectiveness, we could have handled it ourselves. Besides, she couldn't break Oath. Signing the register is legally binding. She would have faced imprisonment here. She could have run under the Capture option, but..."

She leaned back in her chair and said grimly, "We couldn't risk the consequences if she was caught. If the male captures her, she has to obey him sexually for however much of the month is left. He can do what he likes to her, as long as he doesn't hurt her emotionally or physically."

Seeing the hardness in her brother's eyes, she forced a more neutral tone. "A high stakes gamble with possibly intense sexual consequences. For Sharon, it was out of the question. Oh, and with Capture, noncomp papers are out, too. You're stuck."

Gage leaned back in his chair and wiped his hand over his face in an absent-minded gesture of frustration. Obviously, Sharon had made the only choice that she could make, given the options. Suddenly, he remembered something else about Shimerians. He hated to even mention the topic to Kate. She would get upset, but he had to know. "They're psychic, aren't they? Or some form of it?"

Kate knew her face had gone pale at the mention of the word, but she said evenly, "Yes, I think they have some unusual mental abilities. I couldn't find any concrete evidence in my research, but there are too many rumors from too many places." She looked away.

Gage felt the weight of silence hang between them for a long moment. Kate was avoiding looking at him. He decided to confront the issue directly. "Kate, we both know psychic powers are possible. I'm clairvoyant and there's no getting around it. I've proven it enough times in our lives. Just because you don't like what I see, doesn't mean it's not real."

Panic and anger raged inside her, so Kate purposefully turned cool. "It's not that I don't believe in your powers. You know I do. I just don't believe in destiny. You may have seen your..." her voice caught, but she quickly got it under control, "...death, but I refuse to accept it. You're healthy and sitting right here in front of me. Nothing's going to happen."

Gage's heart twisted at the look on his sister's face. She knew deep down that he was right, but she couldn't accept it. Unfortunately, she was going to have to accept it soon. He could sense time running out.

There was a new feeling of urgency lately. The vision was occurring with an alarming frequency now. He had hoped he was overstressed and that a vacation would lessen the feeling and the dreams. Instead, as he'd relaxed, they'd only grown stronger. He could feel his life slipping away, hour by hour. His heart sped up in his chest. Not much longer. There was no doubt.

Watching Kate's pain-filled face, he groped helplessly with a way to comfort her. Pasting on a smile he said lightly, "Come on, Kit-Kate, you know I've lived a life full enough for ten men."

He watched with rising panic as her eyes grew over-bright at the childhood nickname. Kate never cried. This conversation was getting bad in a hurry. Deliberately goading her he said, "Hey, I've single-handedly worked my way through the female population of this city and two foreign cities as well. I don't plan to die until I have at least two more cities under my belt."

Kate knew what he was doing. He was bringing up his playboy image to distract her. Rather than being distracted, she spoke with firm resolve. "I don't care what visions you've had. You're not dying young and that's final." Attempting to lighten the moment, she continued primly, "And psychic visions are no excuse for being oversexed."

Gage couldn't help admiring his sister's determination and control. Kate was one hell of a fighter. He grinned. "Who needs an excuse for being oversexed when it's so much fun?"

Suddenly, there was a loud commotion in the hallway. Gage stood and flashed a warning look at Kate. "Stay here. Something's happening."

Kate ignored her brother and stood as well. Suddenly, the flustered voice of her assistant was heard saying clearly, "But sirs, you can't interrupt her. Ms. Carson is busy. If you'll just allow me to…"

Two hulking Pactreps entered her office, with her worried assistant right behind them murmuring objections and apologies. Seeing Gage tense, she moved quickly to bring things under control. She nodded to her assistant. "Darren, it's okay. I'm willing to see these two *gentlemen*." She placed a sarcastic emphasis on the last word.

Gage arched an eyebrow at her in question. She shook her head slightly and dropped casually into her chair. She watched as Gage moved over to the left, and leaned against the wall. He crossed his arms over his chest. He looked at the Pactreps like a sleepy tiger deciding lazily when to pounce on his meal.

Her assistant backed out of the office with an apologetic look. The Pactreps came to a halt in front of her desk. They were wearing identical black pants and white shirts. They were easily six feet, six inches tall and heavily muscled. They looked more like bodyguards than government paper servers.

Gage watched the change come over his sister. When she leaned back in her chair, eyes glinting like ice, smiling wickedly, he almost felt sorry for the Pactreps. When Kate had that look, there was always hell to pay.

She crossed one leg over the other and said gaily, "Hello, boys. It's been weeks since I saw you last, hasn't it?"

Gage could see the huge men flinch a little and had to stifle an urge to laugh. This was going to be good. When neither man responded, Gage realized it was going to be *really* good.

They seemed to be gathering their courage. Considering his sister was five feet six inches tall and less than half of either of their body weights, the sight of the two hesitant reps was hilarious.

Finally, they had shown up to take her to Sharon, Kate thought gleefully. Her dealings with the Pact Officials this week had been unproductive.

Basically, they had succeeded in convincing her that she would be contacted when Sharon was due to arrive. Any other information she requested was met with bureaucratic jargon and evasion.

Now, she had the same two Pacteps assigned to escort her as last time. When the reps remained silent, she gave them a mocking look. They remembered her well. Good. She arched one smooth eyebrow and said overly pleasantly, "Oh, dear. I'm speaking too fast for you again, aren't I?"

Speaking slowly and carefully, as if to a small child, she said, "Now, what were your names? Oh yes, Everest and Rushmore. Couldn't get me to come to you, so you had to come to me?"

One of the men spoke. "I'm Pactrepresentative Dik si'Dalon and this is Jr. Pactrep Joseph Swann."

Kate nearly broke into laughter at the incongruity of the last name Swann. The rep was a huge hulking creature, and graceful he was not. Of course, he didn't look like anybody's junior anything either. Struggling to keep a straight face, she said, "Let's not make molehills out of mountains, shall we?"

When their faces remained blank, she sighed. Suddenly changing tactics, she demanded in a hard voice, "What do you want? And you'd better not be telling me Sharon is being kept past today. I've read the paperwork and my client will *not* be forcibly detained."

The two men glanced at each other and then Swann spoke in a cautious voice. "Sharon Glaston is returning today. We have the witness order to summon you there. The pledging ceremony is to be held at three o'clock."

Kate sat up, uncrossed her legs, and placed her hands on her desk. In her coldest voice, she challenged, "The hell it will. I notice you're just now notifying me and it's already two-fifteen. Left it a little late there, didn't you Junior?"

He winced, but held his ground. "We are here to notify you of the pledge ceremony and your required presence. In addition, we have more papers to serve."

Taking a step toward Gage, Swann approached him and said, "We have been searching for you. You are her brother, correct?"

Gage watched the man through narrowed eyes. Something was going on here, and he had a sudden feeling it involved Kate and not Sharon. Straightening from the wall, he said coolly, "Yes, I'm Gage Carson. Why?"

The man handed Gage a piece of paper gingerly, as if he was feeding a wild animal. When Gage took the paper, Swann stepped back cautiously. Gage began reading.

Kate watched her brother's brow wrinkle in confusion. As his head came up in surprise, he shot her a stunned look she couldn't interpret. "What is it?" she asked in alarm.

Pactrep si'Dalon stepped in front of her. Suddenly realizing the two men were between her and her brother, she stepped forward until she was within a foot of si'Dalon and glared up at him.

The representative held up another sheet of paper and began to read. "Katherine Harmony Carson," his voice nearly choked on her middle name, but he continued reading in a low steady voice. "You are hereby summoned to Oath by the world government of Shimeria and the..."

"What?!" Kate knew her voice was shrill, but she was shocked to the core. "Did you just say *I've* been summoned to Oath?!"

The representative continued reading as if his very mission in life was to finish the summons. "...and the United Government of..." Gage and Kate began talking at the same time.

"No way in hell," Gage said in a dangerously furious voice. "She's not going. You guys have picked the wrong two women. I'm telling you now--it's not happening."

Kate continued exclaiming, "There is no way that could be right. Do you know what the odds of Sharon and my both being summoned are? Only one in twenty thousand on the register is summoned. The odds of two best friends being called are astronomical. Somebody has screwed up here big time."

Suddenly she heard a familiar name in the midst of the rep's droning. "Wait a second. Did you say the name Tair da'Kamon? As in--a relative of Liken da'Kamon?"

Her mind filled again with the image of the Shimerian male, Liken's brother whom she had met briefly at Sharon's pact ceremony. She knew down to her bones he was the one. His drop-dead good looks were exceeded only by his arrogance.

Remembering his smugly grinning face, she had the sudden impulse to hit something, *hard*. He had known while they were talking that he would summon her to Oath. That knowing light in his eyes and smug attitude made sense now. She felt fury flood her at the mere thought.

The Pactrep's voice stopped finally as he reached the end of the summons. Looking up, he said in a gloating voice, "It is done. You must accompany us to the Pactbuilding for the ceremony." His entire body went tense as if he expected her to spring at him.

Kate's eyelids came down to hide her eyes and her face lost all expression. With a narrow look, she said calmly, "I'll meet you boys there."

Gage made a sudden motion forward, but her pointed look stopped him in his tracks. Studying his sister, he knew she had developed a plan. Deciding to trust her for the moment, he said casually, "I'll transport you."

Both Pactreps shook their heads. Swann said, "You both must accompany us now. It is in the papers."

Kate reached out and took the paper from si'Dalon. Reading it over carefully, she found the clause. He was right. Thinking hard for a minute, she said flatly, "I'll accompany you. We'll notify my partners of what's happening and drop by my house first."

Suddenly, she realized that Sharon would be getting back shortly. Her temper spiked as she realized the timing. She clamped down swiftly on her anger yet again and said coolly, "Or not. I guess you guys have timed it so that I have to leave with you to meet Sharon. Very clever, boys. I never would have suspected an active brain cell between the two of you. Well done."

Swann ignored the insult. "All notifications will be made and procedures followed. The Pactmakers will take care of any necessary details while you are on Shimeria. Everything from plant and pet care to bills to family and work explanations will be handled diligently. You have nothing to fear."

It was the wrong word choice. Kate's back stiffened and she said coldly, "Oh, I'm not afraid. I'm looking forward to having a discussion with Tair. Let's go."

She picked up a stack of papers off her desk and removed her purse from a drawer. She put the papers in her purse with calm efficiency. Slinging it over her shoulder and flashing the two Pactreps a look of disdain, she walked out of the room without a backward glance.

Gage watched his sister walk around the Pactrep and out the door with regal grace and felt like cheering. He knew she had to be panicked at the thought of being summoned, but it didn't show. She had decided to focus her energies on Tair. He knew that sharp brain of hers was busy plotting and planning. Well, he had a few plots of his own. First things first, however.

As Pactrep si'Dilon left in Kate's wake, Gage turned to find Swann regarding him warily. Gage said, "Enjoy your moment of triumph. Kate will be stirring up hell soon enough." Leaning forward until he was within inches of touching the representative, he said, "Of course, you're probably not afraid. Kate has some scruples. She won't blame you for this mess. She knows you're just doing your job."

Gage smiled and grabbed Swann's shirt. He stared hard into the other man's eyes, watching Swann's face grow pale in response. He kept his voice low and even as he continued, "I, on the other hand, don't give a damn about scruples."

He released the man's shirt and leaned back. He said matter-of-factly, "Fuck scruples. Whoever hurts them will pay no matter how small their part in this scheme. If Sharon or Kate suffers, there's no planet in existence where you'll ever be safe." He stepped around the Pactrep and strolled out of the office.

Swann stood there a moment in the silence of the room. The icy threat he had seen in those eyes had been chilling. He knew Gage's background. He felt like he had escaped death by an inch. With absolute certainty he knew Gage's words were true. He sighed.

Some men, he reflected, were like cobras. If you tangled with them, one of you most likely ended up dead. There were days when his job really sucked. With weary steps, he moved to follow the others. Government servants never got any respect.

Chapter 2

Tair da'Kamon stood in the Pactbuilding laughing and talking with Liken and Sharon, but his eyes kept wandering to the doorway of the room. He knew he had to get his restless anticipation under control. Energy was radiating outward from him in waves.

The happy couple beside him was completely oblivious, but the half dozen Shimerian males in the room were regarding him warily. He glanced at the doorway again just as a blonde-haired human male walked through it. He narrowed his eyes thoughtfully, wondering why he looked familiar.

Sharon turned in the direction of the man, obviously puzzled by what was holding Tair's attention. Suddenly, she shrieked, "Gage!" She broke away from Liken's embrace and rushed toward the newcomer. He caught her in a tight hug, grinning widely and looking relieved. When he pulled back from her, his face was a picture of tenderness and concern.

Tair felt his brother stiffen and take an angry step forward. Tair put a restraining hand on his arm as a precaution and said quietly, "Wait, brother, before doing something you will regret."

Liken relaxed somewhat, but struggled with his control. As he felt the waves of Sharon's warmth and caring for the man wash over him, he worked to suppress his jealousy and sort out all the emotion. Regaining control, he realized she regarded the man as a brother.

With a smile of satisfaction, Liken said, "I am fine, Tair. You persist in treating me as if our age difference was ten years instead of two."

Tair laughed. "I will be older and wiser always. Besides, I am not blinded by love."

Liken saw Tair freeze as a feminine figure walked through the doorway and immediately embraced Sharon. Tair's impatient hunger was obvious in every line of his stance.

Liken snorted and said, "Yet. You are not blinded by love *yet*." Realizing his brother did not even hear his words, he added, "Of course, I could be mistaken. You may love her already."

Ignoring his brother's nonsense, Tair studied Kate as she talked excitedly with Sharon and the blonde-haired man. When the man casually slung his arm across Kate's shoulder in a reassuring gesture, Tair felt jealous anger mix with his already roiling emotions. He took one aggressive step forward just as Liken placed a restraining hand on his arm.

Liken didn't bother hiding his amusement. "So quickly you lose all wisdom. You might consider taking your own advice, brother."

Tair shot him a furious glare and turned to narrowly regard Kate. She looked incredible. Her long, pale blonde hair was swept up in a tight knot at the nape of her neck. Her blue eyes were wide as she talked animatedly with Sharon. She was wearing a red blouse, with black pants and high heels. She looked professional and composed, and beyond lovely. He went rock hard in an instant. Suddenly, she turned toward him as if sensing his hungry gaze. Their eyes met with an almost physical clash.

* * * * *

Kate paused outside of the Pactroom doorway in the hallway and felt a moment of total panic. She had ditched the annoying Pactreps after they walked her into the building. She was grateful to be alone for a moment. She had persuaded Gage to go ahead and check on Sharon. She wanted to enter the Pactroom by herself, fearless and independent-- not looking like she needed a strong male beside her.

She felt her heart lodge in her throat as she thought about facing Tair. Thinking about him in the abstract, even dreaming about him was one thing, but live and in the flesh was something else altogether. His image flashed through her mind yet again.

He was so intensely male. He had curly black hair and those incredible blue eyes. He was so big. And that lean and muscular body--she hastily veered from the thought. Better to remember those piercing blue eyes.

She remembered his gaze roaming her body possessively at Sharon's Oath ceremony. He had a way of looking at her as if they were one step from the bedroom. A little hum of aroused anticipation ran through her. Okay, forget his eyes, too.

She gave an exasperated groan. This would never do. She would be lost before it started if she didn't find her backbone fast. *Kate Carson is a killer attorney* she reminded herself. *She's powerful, and in control, and has never met a man who could best her in any arena. Bedroom or boardroom, she walks away smiling. Always.*

She had to help Sharon and she had to face Tair. Tair was no different from any other man, she chided inwardly. He might affect her in strange ways, and he might be from another planet, but in the end, after all, he was just a man.

Taking a deep breath and squaring her shoulders, she walked into the room like a soldier sure of winning the battle -- and went weak with relief as she saw Sharon wrapped in Gage's arms. Sharon was really here and okay. Joy filled her. Sharon saw her and held out her arms.

With a happy smile Kate came forward and hugged Sharon hard. Fighting the wild surge of emotion, she worked on keeping her composure. Leaning back, Kate said shakily, "All this excessive emotion. And you know how I detest physical displays."

Sharon laughed and hugged her a second time, even harder. Pulling away, she chided, "Don't think for one second I believe you. I know better. It's me. I know how mushy you can get."

Kate grinned widely and struggled to give Sharon a look of mock reproof. "Not so loudly, please. I have a reputation to uphold." Pulling back to look into her friend's face more closely, she was startled to see the unmistakable glow of happiness on Sharon's face.

No, more than happiness, Sharon looked radiant. Whatever had happened in Shimeria had actually been good for her friend. The cold feeling of dread that had lived inside her since Sharon left, drained away. She laughed with delighted relief. "You look wonderful. I gather interplanetary nookie agrees with you."

Feeling her brother shift uncomfortably beside her, she turned a mocking look on him. "Gage, darling, you do realize she's had sex before? I myself have even been known to indulge."

Gage gave her a look that promised retribution. With a glare of disapproval at her, he said, "No, and I don't want to realize it now. The two of you date but you do *not* have sex. Trust me when I tell you in this case, ignorance is bliss."

Rolling her eyes and laughing at her brother, Kate said, "How very typically male. Too fragile to deal with the harsh realities of life."

Sharon piped up at that moment, "Actually, Liken is fantastic." When Gage winced and Kate arched an eyebrow she added hurriedly, "I didn't mean sex. Well, yes, the sex is unbelievable..."

She broke off at the pained look on Gage's face and gave a choked laugh. "I meant Liken is a wonderful man."

Eying her friend skeptically, Kate said, "Honey, that's sex talking. The stud of the universe must have come through for you in a big way."

Sharon grew more solemn and said quietly, "Actually, Kate, that's love talking. I'm in love with him and I'm going to pledge with him today."

Kate felt like she'd been hit with a large object with no warning. She felt Gage put a reassuring arm across her shoulders even as they both tensed. This was an unexpected development. There was a pregnant pause, as Kate searched for a response.

"Sharon," she began carefully, "I respect your feelings, but I'm wondering about his. Does he love you, too?" She couldn't completely keep the doubt from her voice.

Sharon smiled and her voice was firm. There was confidence and something close to pride in her face. "Yes, he does. We've found something together, Kate--something very rare. I have so much to tell you, so much to explain." Sharon frowned. "Actually, I think I need to tell you some of those things right now."

Suddenly, Kate became aware of Tair standing across the room. She had no idea how she knew it, but she knew it. She turned toward him instinctively, and then realized what she was doing and turned back. She could feel him staring at her, but refused to look his way.

She was too aware of him, she thought with alarm. It was not a good sign. Finally, giving in to the impulse, she turned and looked at him. Their gazes locked and she felt her breath catch.

He was looking at her with focused intensity, as if the entire world had narrowed to the two of them. Holding his gaze, she refused to look away. They stared at each for a long moment. Then, she heard Sharon's voice. Breaking the impasse, she turned and looked at her friend, trying to get back into the conversation.

Still, a thrill went through her as she realized they would start battling soon. It was almost time. She tried to suppress her rising excitement. Refocusing on Sharon, she asked, "I need to know what?" On the edge of her vision, she could still see

Tair. He was crossing the room with powerful strides.

He reached their small group just as Sharon said, "You need to know about..."

"The ceremony will be beginning soon, Sharon," Tair drawled in a deceptively lazy voice, but there was a note of warning, too. "Perhaps I should tell Kate the necessary details. I imagine Liken would like his presence remembered as well."

Sharon shot him a guilty look, laced with defiance. "Liken is perfectly fine. I think Kate and I need to have a little talk before either ceremony begins."

Kate knew she looked surprised. "You know I've been summoned?" How long had Sharon known? For that matter, how long had Tair known?

Watching as Tair laid an arm across Sharon's shoulders, she wondered at the look exchanged between the two. He hugged her, as if to indicate he was not truly angry. There was a casual intimacy, as well as affection between Sharon and Tair that was surprising. They acted like old friends.

Gage stepped forward and pulled Sharon away from Tair with gentle firmness. Staring hard at the Shimerian, he challenged coldly, "I'm Gage Carson. Who are you?"

Tair realized why Gage looked so familiar. Kate and Gage had the same blond good looks. Seeing the two of them so close together, it was unmistakable. The resemblance between the siblings was obvious now. He mentally rolled his eyes at his own foolishness.

His hostility toward the other man lessened considerably. Sensing the anger emanating from Gage, he reminded himself that Gage was Kate's brother. Tair held his hard gaze but said in a neutral tone, "I am Tair da'Kamon."

Liken joined the group at that moment. Sharon shot a worried glance at the two men staring so hard at each other, and then raised her eyes to Liken in an unconscious plea. Liken gave her a reassuring smile and reached out for her.

Drawing her close to his side, he said to Gage in a jovial voice, "I am Liken da'Kamon, Sharon's pactmate. Sharon has great affection for you. I am most pleased you could come to our pledging." Liken extended his hand toward Gage.

Gage turned his attention from Tair and focused on Liken. He gave him a lethal glare, until he glanced at Sharon. Seeing the plea in her eyes, he sighed uncomfortably.

Finally, thrusting his hand out, he took Liken's hand in a brief shake. It wasn't particularly friendly, but it was a gesture of temporary truce. Sharon gave him a grateful smile.

Kate stood silently watching the drama unfold. It looked like any physical altercation had been averted, at least for the moment. Deciding the timing was good, she took a step forward and said in a chilly voice, "Hello, Tair."

Tair grinned widely at the tone and said in an amused drawl, "Hello, Kate."

They stared at each other silently. The others in the group said nothing as the air became even more charged. The connection between Kate and Tair was nearly tangible. Even the Shimerian males waiting in line along the side of the room shifted restlessly, watching with interested eyes.

They were Shimerian males of various ages and backgrounds, but they had one thing in common. They were all in line to make Pact arrangements. Some had seen a Pact ceremony at one time or another, but most had not. They were curious about the two couples and the ceremony. Liken and his pactmate were pledging, but Tair was about to take Oath.

Tair was a highly respected Guardian with quite a reputation for power. They were curious about the woman who would become his mate. Then everyone froze as another Shimerian male entered the room. They turned toward each other and several murmured, "Jadik" in surprise to the others.

Kate watched as the most gorgeous man she'd ever laid eyes on walked toward them. He was big, with black hair falling down to his wide shoulders. His face was... the only word to describe it was beautiful. Like a painting of a dark angel, she'd seen once in a museum. As his gaze landed on her, she suppressed a shiver of alarm.

He might be gorgeous, but this man was deadly. Those brown eyes were calculating and hard as stone. He silently assessed her as he drew near. She felt like he was seeing all the way to her soul. Then, his look changed to one of appreciation. As his eyes drifted over her body, she felt unaccountably warm.

This reaction was not good. Was she turning into some kind of sex-crazed maniac all of the sudden? First Tair and now this man. She did not like what was happening one bit.

Tair made a welcoming gesture toward him and said, "Jadik, your sense of timing is impeccable as always."

Kate watched in surprise as Jadik's face relaxed and he smiled. It transformed his whole face, making him look deceptively harmless. "Hello, Tair. You know I would not miss the ceremony. Ahh... Liken it is good to see you again."

His gaze turned gently mocking as it landed on Sharon. He said, "I see you have decided to keep the idiot after all."

Sharon's face turned bright red in response. Jadik threw back his head and laughed at her reaction. "Don't look so embarrassed, *sherree*. I remember that night rather fondly." His gaze fell to her mouth and then drifted upward as he gave her a lazy wink.

Sharon cleared her throat and sought desperately for a response. "Hi, Jadik. Umm... This is my best friend, Kate, and her brother Gage."

Gage nodded shortly at Jadik and turned his attention back to Tair. In a light voice, completely at odds with his grim expression, he said suddenly, "Tair, I don't believe we've shaken hands." He thrust his hand out toward the other man.

The entire group regarded Gage in surprised confusion for a moment. Then Kate's brow cleared as she realized what was happening and she said, "Yes, that's right. Tair, you should shake hands with Gage."

Tair studied the other man for a moment in silence and then took the offered hand. As their hands touched, Tair was shocked by the sudden flood of energy that erupted. Instinctively, he shielded his mind and sent an answering probe toward Gage's mind to discover what he intended. To his astonishment, he met with a shield. It was not a Shimerian mind shield, but it was somewhat similar.

Gage gasped and held on as the world around him went gray. He rarely tried to force a vision because the drain was so great. He risked passing out whenever he tried. In this case, he needed to know and he needed to know right now. A great deal depended on his abilities at the moment. As a series of images passed through his mind, he felt a surge of relief. Then, suddenly, he burst into laughter.

Tair broke Gage's grip and studied the man in stunned silence. No one spoke as Gage continued to laugh so hard that his shoulders shook.

When the storm of laughter subsided, Tair said, "You are psychic. Yet you are human. I do not understand."

Sharon and Kate looked alarmed. Sharon said immediately, "Keep your voice down, Tair. It's not a common natural ability here."

Tair said in a low tone, "My apologies, Gage. I am usually discrete. I was merely surprised."

Gage grinned widely, amusement still evident in his face. "Oh, that's okay, pal. You'll be *really* sorry soon enough."

Tair knew when he was being taunted, but there was a genuine lessening of hostility from

Gage. Even a note of camaraderie. It was mocking, but it was there.

With a puzzled frown, he decided humans were too confusing to understand fully. Turning to Kate, he said, "Kate, I must speak with you now. It is…" He stopped abruptly at Sharon's exclamation.

Sharon voice rang loudly with disbelief. "Jadik! You have *got* to be kidding. Kate, I just thought of something. No, I know it can't be right. Tair, tell me Jadik is not Kate's…"

Before she could say the word, Liken placed his mouth over hers in an enthusiastic kiss. When he raised his head, he said firmly, "Sharon, I believe Tair and Kate have things to discuss."

"But Jadik?!" she exclaimed. "Tell me I'm wrong."

Liken said to the group, "Please excuse us, we have pledge details to discuss." He shot a hard look at Sharon, who returned it with an even harder one of her own.

Finally, nodding her head in agreement, she said, "Excuse us, we'll just be a moment." The couple strode over to the other side of the room and began speaking in low tones.

Kate gave Jadik a questioning glance, but he merely shrugged and looked angelically innocent. She wasn't fooled for a second.

Turning to Tair, she said firmly, "I believe we'll have that discussion now." Walking out of the room and into the outside corridor, she was surprised when Tair turned into one of the doorways instead of following her further down the hall.

Rolling her eyes that he couldn't even follow her to the lobby, she turned and followed him into an office of some kind. Except for the two of them, it was empty. The owner of the office must be gone for the day because everything looked too neat and tidy for ongoing work. There was a desk with a built-in computer monitor and a chair. Tair was sitting on the edge of the desk looking as if he didn't have a care in the world.

Against her will, her gaze drifted downward toward his lap. As her eyes reached their destination, she saw a thick bulge against his crotch. She jerked her eyes upward and met his amused regard. With a defiant toss of her head, she demanded, "You wanted to talk. Fine. Talk. Explain this ridiculous summoning."

Tair smiled. "Kate, there is no need for this battle. If you wish it, I am willing to take the Oath of Seduction. Seducing you would be pure pleasure."

Kate felt her insides grow warm at his words. Moisture gathered between her thighs. His gaze drifted downward to fall on her breasts. Even though she was completely covered by her suit, she felt naked. Her nipples tightened in response.

His eyes drifted back to her face and he said in a husky voice, "Of course, you may seduce me if that is your desire."

Kate struggled for control. It was infuriating that he could affect her so quickly and so strongly. With renewed resolve, she asked pointedly, "And if I choose one of the other options?"

He straightened from the desk and stalked toward her. Her excitement rose with each step.

When he was inches away from touching her, he spoke softly, his voice a combination of temptation and subtle dare. "If you choose Challenge, you have my oath that I will not harm you, but I *will* challenge you sexually."

Reaching out, he ran his hand gently along the curve of her neck. It was a causally intimate gesture. His voice held the same tone, as his hand stroked. "Think of it, Kate. What games we can play! You can explore your every desire with me. There is nothing that I would not do to you, nothing that you could not have from me."

Reaching the neckline of her blouse, he dipped a finger lazily between the curves of her breasts. "I will fulfill you in ways you have experienced only in your deepest fantasies. Imagine what we could do to each other."

Kate tried to keep from trembling at his words, but she felt a tremor run through her. Her body was heating, the blood singing in her veins. The man was a master. Clenching her hands, she said coolly, "You presume a lot. I hope you have the equipment and skill to match that huge ego."

He chuckled and began placing kisses along the side of her throat. His fingers began tracing circles over her breast. Her body tensed in anticipation, but he avoided her aching nipple. He said huskily, "You are welcome to verify it at any time."

He bit gently at the spot where her neck met her shoulder, then sucked. His hand covered her breast and squeezed. Through the fabric of her blouse, the contact of his warm palm with her hard nipple was exquisite.

It was too much temptation. Kate groaned and grabbed for his head with both hands. Pulling his face up, she placed a hungry kiss on his mouth. His lips hardened instantly and began moving in response. She felt him his big arms wrap around her, and then he pulled her fully against the hard length of his body.

They both groaned as the contact sent fire arching through them. Their tongues met eagerly in a passionate duel as the kiss grew hotter. Kate felt Tair's cock thrusting aggressively against her stomach and arched upward, trying to align her sex with that hard pressure.

Immediately, Tair's hands slid to her butt and lifted her. As he thrust against her sex for the first time, she moaned loudly and felt her whole body shudder. She wrapped her legs around him and heard him moan. She was burning. They were both on fire.

Then, suddenly, she felt a pressure inside her head. It was a pressing sensation, like something was pushing against her mind. She was jolted out of the moment, and immediately pulled back from Tair.

Tair's eyes were black with desire. His mouth was swollen and he looked ready to eat her alive. Kate knew she looked the same way. Pushing against his shoulders, she unwrapped her legs from around his body.

He looked dazed at her sudden withdrawal, but he allowed her body to slide down until she stood on her own. He murmured, "I want you, Kate."

In desperation, she turned her back on him and walked on shaky legs a few steps away. Breathing harshly, she tried to engage her brain. She needed to think, and she needed to do it fast. He had barely touched her and she'd gone off like a rocket. It was scary and incredible and the most fantastic sexual thrill of her life.

He spoke roughly from behind her, sounding impatient. "What happened?"

She spun and flashed him an angry look, "Why don't you tell me? You're the one with the superhero powers, remember?"

A look of resignation passed over his face. Taking a deep breath and letting it out, he shrugged. "My apologies for losing control. It is quite common the first time one kisses his pactmate."

Kate felt a surge of irritation at the thought of what had almost happened. She decided it was time to go on the offensive. She needed to settle down and take control. Immediately. She reached for icy composure.

Keeping her face bland and her voice cool, she walked until they were nearly touching again. Reaching out and touching his big chest, she could literally feel his heart pounding, even through his shirt. Trailing a finger down his chest, she watched the hunger in his face grow. She lingered at the top of his pants and then moved her palm further down over his crotch.

"Well," she drawled softly, "you can make it up to me." She stroked a gentle hand over his cock and then cupped him in her hand. Inwardly, she groaned at the feel of him, so huge and so ready. A cock like that was enough to make any woman beg.

Outwardly, she flashed him a teasing smile. "We'll enjoy each other for two lovely weeks." She stroked him slowly, trying to distance herself from the pleasure of that hard length in her hand. "Then I'll come back home. Imagine how incredible it could be, Tair."

She licked her lips, and watched with satisfaction as his eyes tracked her movements. She trailed her hand down all the way to his inner thigh and then went upward until she cupped his testicles gently. In a firmer voice, she said, "But no intercourse and no mind stuff, darling."

Tair was in agony. Kate was fighting back with a vengeance. His entire body was aching with the desire to take her. His cock throbbed in her hand and he grasped for control. He shook his head in the negative.

The hand cupping him tightened slowly in response. She stopped squeezing just short of pain. Tair sucked in a breath and went absolutely still.

Kate smiled in satisfaction. She remembered to keep her voice cool and mocking. "Well, that really is too bad. I'm warning you, Romeo, no more mind tricks or you'll pay. Challenge me and you'll lose." Abruptly, she released him and stepped quickly out of his reach.

Tair regarded her silently for a moment. He let out a deep breath as he struggled with his temper. Then, with a casual shrug, he turned and leaned against the desk. He wanted her more fiercely than his next breath, and he was determined not to give her the satisfaction of knowing it.

Finally, he said equally coolly, "I will not accommodate you."

Kate watched in silence as his shoulders relaxed, but his face turned resolute. He appeared calm and in control, but there was a dangerous look in his eyes. His voice was hard. "I intend to merge with you as soon as possible."

"As for intercourse," he lifted one brow in obvious amusement and continued matter-of-factly, "We will have sex, Kate, you may depend upon it. I will have you wet and wanting, and aching for my cock. Then, I will fuck you mindless. You will pledge with me, *sheka*. You have my oath."

Kate was rocked by what he said. His blunt words excited and angered her at the same time. Seething with frustration, arousal, and anger, she said with frigid precision, "You have my oath you'll regret the day you ever met me. I have to change my clothes. I have two ceremonies to attend." Giving him a look of dismissal, she turned and stalked out of the room.

Tair leaned on the corner of the desk for another moment. As his arousal dimmed and his mind cleared, he threw back his head and laughed at the two of them. They were both tough players. They were both used to winning. And they were very well-matched indeed. Gradually, his laughter subsided into a smugly satisfied grin. She would choose Challenge. He was sure of it. Kate was ready to play.

Chapter 3

Kate stood in the small changing room gazing at herself in the mirror with disgust. She was dressed in a thin white blouse, and a floor length skirt of matching material. Tiny flat strappy sandals and skimpy panties that tied at the hips completed the outfit. She looked like some kind of virginal sacrifice. She felt utterly ridiculous. She could imagine the reactions of her co-workers if they glimpsed this getup.

She remembered seeing the same type of outfit on Sharon weeks ago, but on Sharon it had looked beautiful and appropriate somehow. Very "innocence on the verge of blossoming" or something. Looking at her thrusting nipples outlined by the cloth, Kate felt like a hooker dressed as a nun.

She was no innocent in body or in mind. Glancing at her red and black power suit hanging on the hook on the wall, she gave it an approving look. That suit was Kate Carson. This virginal bride thing was a bad joke.

Coming to a decision, she reached up and loosened her hair. Brushing her hands through it, she watched it fall in loose waves past her shoulders. Spotting her purse in the corner, she gave a small grimace. Actually, she had left it in the

Pactrep's transport. No doubt one of the mountains had retrieved it for her and put it in here.

Reaching for it, she drew out a tube of lipstick. The color was 'Killer Red." She used it on her lips and stood back to assess the effect. With her hair down and her kiss-swollen lips painted deep crimson, she looked rather wanton. The flush from her encounter with Tair earlier only added to the image. Her eyes were shining with heated emotion.

She didn't look like anybody's innocent sacrifice now. She looked like a woman completely comfortable with her own sexuality. Powerful and challenging. Perfect. She hoped Tair would be in major agony. It served him right.

Picking up her red purse, she smiled to herself. It was going to be a very pleasurable two weeks. If he thought she'd just roll over for him, he was badly mistaken. She'd take her fun where she found it, and walk away smiling – alone -- at the end.

Somehow the thought didn't please her as much as it should. It was that damn intergalactic jerk. He was unlike anyone she had ever encountered. A part of her knew she would miss the intensity of their effect on each other once the knowing period was done.

Then again, maybe they would grow bored with each other. Anything that blazed this hot was bound to burn out fast. With a mental shrug at her mixed emotions, she took one last look in the mirror.

She was Kate Carson, powerful and in control. Hell-on-wheels and a woman to be reckoned with.

It was time to introduce Tair to the concept of humility.

Walking out into the Pactroom, there was a sudden hush. Feeling everyone's gaze on her, she met their eyes boldly and searched for Sharon. Tair was missing. Trust the damn man to miss her big entrance.

Feeling somewhat deflated, she spotted Sharon gesturing to her. Kate smiled and went to her friend. For the first time, she really became aware of what Sharon was wearing. The halter top and short skirt looked wonderful on her.

Studying Sharon, Kate realized her friend looked sexy and confident. There was a new contentment about her, a kind of inner satisfaction. If Liken had this effect, Kate could forgive him a lot.

The big alien was looking at Sharon in absolute adoration. Obviously feeling Liken's gaze on her, Sharon turned and returned the look for a moment. They both smiled.

Kate, watching the two, felt a moment of envy. They were deeply in love. She might doubt her own capacity for the emotion, but there was no mistaking the feeling between Sharon and Liken. It was there in the tenderness between them. They seemed to have a special...knowledge of each other, a bond. Even someone who had never felt that kind of love could identify it easily.

Dread surfaced at the thought of being so far from her friend. With a bittersweet smile, she realized things were changing. Sharon would be leaving to live so far away. She felt a huge sadness take hold.

Intense loneliness swamped her at the thought. She shook herself inwardly. The bottom line was Sharon was happy, and she wanted that happiness for her friend. If it meant Liken and another planet, Kate would wish them well.

Pasting a smile on her face, she said in her best disapproving tone, "Please, this lovey-dovey stuff is wreaking hell on my nerves. You two need to have a fight or something so I'll feel more comfortable. Exchange a few insults or glares. I need something more suited to my personality. It is my Oath ceremony, too, you know."

Liken gave her a confident smile, surprising her, and said, "Kate, I have been inside Sharon's head. As much as it will pain you, I know you through her eyes. You cannot hope to fool me with such talk."

Sharon laughed. Kate gave him a hard glare for a moment. With cool accents she said, "I see Sharon loves you in spite of your delusional thinking. It's so sad when love makes fools out of intelligent men."

Liken reached out and enveloped her in a hug. She stiffened in shock for a moment and then relaxed. His arms around her felt comforting and for a minute, she leaned into the embrace. Then, regretting the temporary weakness, she moved back.

He was looking at her warmly. He leaned down and placed a gentle buss on her mouth, as if she were a child. Eyes shining with amusement, he said, "Kate, love makes fools of us all."

Leaning down, he whispered in her ear, "You will never lose her. I swear it on my life. She will know happiness with me, but you will always be a part of her life as well." He chucked her under the chin, and moved back to Sharon's side.

Kate stood in shock, marveling over the big alien's words and actions. He had somehow guessed what she was feeling and had made the effort to comfort her. It meant more to her than she would ever let him know.

She cleared her throat. "Sharon, you are allowed to keep this pathetic creature. Obviously he will do anything for you, even attempt to befriend me."

Flashing him a look, she said, "You'll do. Just don't expect that hugging thing to occur very often." She gave a delicate shudder of mock revulsion.

Liken and Sharon both burst into laughter. Kate smiled widely in response. She heard an excited murmur around the room and felt an intense stare directed her way. Tair was back.

Turning, she saw Tair, Gage, and Jadik walking toward her. Arching an eyebrow, she waited until the three of them arrived. Then she said overly sweetly, "Hello, boys. All done discussing the womenfolk?"

The three men grinned at her and nodded yes. She felt her blood start to boil. She opened her mouth to make a scathing response.

The voice of the Pactmaker suddenly rang loudly in the room. "Will Liken da'Kamon and Sharon Glaston please step forward to pledge?"

Liken caught Sharon by the hand and led her forward. Tair reached a hand toward Kate, but she merely stared at it like an unwelcome reptile. With a laugh, he moved his hand forward in a gesture for her to proceed first. Turning her back on him, she walked toward the Pactmaker. She missed the three amused male smiles that she left in her wake.

Eventually, everyone gathered into the appropriate places for the ceremony. Sharon and Liken faced each other, with Kate and Tair standing on each side. Jadik and Gage stood further away, watching silently. Gage regarded Sharon with the wistful eyes of a brother sending off his little sister. The couple gave their Oaths in clear, solemn voices. Their happiness and joy were evident.

Kate tried to concentrate on the pledge ceremony. The beauty of it didn't escape her, but her mind was a jumble of thoughts. Her emotions were cascading from happiness for Sharon and Liken, to apprehension about Tair and the ceremony to follow.

Unused to such a mix of strong emotions, she worked hard to keep her composure. If her eyes became a little misty when Liken placed a gentle kiss on Sharon's mouth as the beauty of it truly touched her, she made sure no one noticed by looking quickly away. At last it was done.

Feeling Tair's gaze, she turned and gave him a look of warning. He held her look for a moment, but she could have sworn there was tenderness in those eyes. Then, everyone was hugging everyone, and the moment was lost.

Amidst the confusion of laughter and well wishes, the Pactmaker spoke again. "Will Tair da'Kamon and Katherine Carson step forward to take the Oath please?"

Kate felt a moment of pure panic as her heart leapt into her throat. Tair stepped in front of her and leaned down to whisper, "You are not thinking of running, *sheka*? Scared so soon? I thought you wanted to play?"

Kate felt her temper leap. Her composure returned. With a lazy hand she smoothed her blouse. With careful calculation, she watched as his eyes were drawn to her tight nipples. When his hungry gaze returned to her face, she said with a smug smile, "Excuse me, clueless. You're in my way."

He smiled appreciatively. "My apologies once again. Let us proceed."

He turned and she followed until the two of them faced each other in front of the Pactmaker. She was surprised to see Jadik step forward behind Tair, as Liken moved back. Sharon came to stand behind her. Gage and Liken waited side by side. The Shimerian males in line along the wall watched with fascination. She gave Tair a puzzled glance. He merely shrugged and said, "It is customary."

Feeling more confused than enlightened by his statement, she wondered what the hell was going on. There was some significance to Jadik's position, but she wasn't going to get any answers from Tair. The Pactmaker began speaking then and she tried to focus on his words.

With a feeling of total unreality, she realized she was in effect getting engaged to an alien. The whole idea was preposterous, but it was actually happening. As the Pactmaker droned on, she ignored him as she realized she had heard it just three weeks before, when Sharon took the Oath.

She concentrated on keeping her expression closed and her panic hidden. Her heart was pounding in her chest but she was not going to let anyone see her fear. When the Pactmaker asked for her choice, she shot a defiant look at Tair and said clearly, "I choose Challenge."

Tair grinned broadly and promptly kneeled at her feet. She was utterly shocked at his action. He lifted his head and explained, "My kneeling is a symbol, Kate. When I stand again, it means I have accepted your challenge."

As the Pactmaker continued talking, Kate studied Tair. He didn't look humbled by his position at all. If anything, he seemed amused.

She leaned down a little and taunted in a low voice, "You look good on your knees."

He laughed and whispered back, "Best to remember the sight fondly when I have *you* on yours."

With a glare, she snorted and realized the Pactmaker was no longer talking. Suddenly, Tair stood with easy grace and gazed down at her from his superior height. His gaze swept her body boldly, with absolute possession. With satisfied eyes and a cocky grin, he spoke his own Oath.

Kate didn't even hear the words. Tair's look had pretty much stunned her. Her breath caught when he stood, and she couldn't seem to get it back. He was actually going to give her whatever she wanted sexually. She knew it down to her bones.

The possibilities of the next few weeks flashed through her mind. Growing more aroused by the second, she couldn't seem to focus on what he was saying. With a deep breath, she looked away, closing her eyes. Then, Tair caught her chin in his hands, and planted a brief hard kiss on her mouth. The ceremony was done.

She opened her eyes slowly and peered into his face. His expression looked tender, but changed instantly to hungry desire. With a muttered oath, he leaned down and gave her a second, more thorough kiss. When they drew apart, they were breathing hard.

Jadik's voice penetrated their involvement with each other. "Tair, my apologies, but I must go. I have obligations that cannot wait. My congratulations to you both."

Tair reached out and placed one hand on Jadik's shoulder as Jadik mirrored him with the opposite hand. Kate presumed it was the Shimerian form of a handshake. Jadik made a movement toward her next. She looked at him and said sternly, "No. There's something about you that's not right. You don't fool me. And do *not* congratulate me for getting engaged to this smug idiot, please."

Jadik laughed loudly. "Beauty and spirit in one small body, along with the solid instincts of a good player. Tair has quite a challenge to enjoy. *Sherree*, it will be my pleasure to see more of you on Shimeria soon."

He had emphasized the word "pleasure." She eyed him suspiciously. He gave her a dazzling smile of pure innocence that nearly melted her in her shoes. She glared in response. He winked at her, nodded at Tair, and then walked away.

Gage moved forward and swept Kate into his arms for a long hug. His arms tightened about her as if he wanted to keep her there forever, and then he pulled back. Kate was shocked at the strained emotion on his face. He looked so sad, almost resigned. It hurt her to see it.

With great tenderness, he brushed the hair off of her face and said solemnly, "Kate, I love you, you know that don't you? And I wouldn't let you go with him if I didn't know he was a good man. No matter what happens on Shimeria, I want you to remember how proud I am to have you as my sister. And there's no one I love more than you in this world or any other. Be happy."

Kate started to tremble. With blurry eyes and a trembling lip, she said, "Oh, that is so unfair. You know I love you, too, Gage. Promise me you'll take care until I'm back to hound you about it myself."

Gage grinned, though his eyes were a little misty. "Of course."

Tair placed a comforting hand on Kate's shoulder. She looked up at him in surprise. With clear reluctance he said gently, "Kate, I am sorry. It is time for us to go."

Sharon and Liken were being led away by the Pactmaker to get their new pledge records done. Sharon broke away from Liken and ran to Kate. Hugging her hard, she said, "I love you, Kate. Have fun. I'll be there for you when we return."

Kate was surprised. "You aren't coming back now?"

Sharon looked briefly guilty. "I need to get the details taken care of here for the move to Shimeria. I may still be here when you get back. There's so much to do." With sudden indecision, she asked, "Do you need me to go with you?"

Kate felt a touch of panic. It really was going to be her and Tair on a completely unknown planet. Shrugging the feeling off, she said firmly, "Of course not. I'll be fine. You did it, didn't you? And you survived perfectly fine."

Throwing a look Liken's way, she said, "Better than fine. Don't worry about me. I'll see you soon."

She hugged Sharon one last time and then stepped back briskly. In a more composed voice, she said, "All this sentimentality is getting maudlin. I could have sworn I had new worlds to conquer. If everyone will quit dawdling I should be able to manage it and be back before dinner."

Sharon laughed and blew her a kiss as she walked back to Liken. Turning, Kate saw Gage and Tair sporting identical grins. Gage laughed and said, "That's my Kate, hell-on-wheels." Planting a kiss on her cheek and with one last lingering look, he turned and walked out of the room.

Kate and Tair were left standing, staring at each other. It was time to go to Shimeria. It was time to begin the Challenge.

Chapter 4

Kate said in a brisk voice, "Let's go." She was feeling the strain of too many emotional moments and shocks. She wasn't exactly in the best state to travel to another planet. She was feeling raw and far more vulnerable than she liked. It was out of character and uncomfortable.

Tair nodded and walked toward the door of the Pactroom. Kate started after him with determined steps, refusing to give in to her mounting apprehension. She was made of sterner stuff. A trip to another planet and a few sexual bouts with an alien weren't going to shake her composure and make her look like a fool.

The two of them were strangely silent as they went down stairs and finally reached a doorway. Following Tair inside, she nearly gasped upon seeing the gigantic portals but managed to keep walking.

They got in line behind others, all waiting to go through customs and enter the portal. Neither broke the other's silent thoughts, as if reluctant to begin. Kate wondered if maybe *both* of them were struggling with nerves, not just her.

Suddenly, Tair turned and handed Kate a small card. Seeing her name and then words in other languages, she asked, "What's this? Some kind of ID card?"

"Yes, it is your card," he said in friendly tones. "I have made all of the arrangements for your arrival on Shimeria. It has a multitude of purposes."

She arched an eyebrow in silent question.

He continued, "In addition to your identification, it is used to purchase goods. You give your card to a merchant and he uses it to deduct money from our account. We have a computer at home tied into central computers. I will show you how it works."

"Oh, *we* do?" she said with emphasis. "*We* seem to be good at details. Do *we* know the details of how these portals work?"

Kate had heard of portals but never imagined she would see one, much less go through one. Wishing she had paid more attention in science class, she viewed the large gates with apprehension. With her luck she'd probably need algebra next. She swallowed. Interplanetary travel was starting to feel real.

Tair gave an unconcerned shrug. "I have no idea. I am unfamiliar with the actual process. It has to do with energy transfer, but beyond that I do not know."

"The other portal to the right," he gestured to the other identical two-story oval structure around which was built some kind of metallic gate, "is for travelers from Shimeria to Earth."

Kate watched as people appeared out of the dense blackness at the center of the hole. Many of the men were Shimerian-sized and they seemed to be traveling alone. However, a few of them gathered in twos or threes after passing the customs officer. To Kate, they had the unmistakable air of boys out on the town.

There were some women also who arrived through the portal alone, but most were paired up rather quickly with a male companion. They all appeared unharmed by their trip through the machine, but Kate was not entirely reassured.

As the line moved forward, she studied the large structure in front of her. It looked big, and black, and distinctly forbidding. The customs officer finished looking at Tair's ID card and turned to her. He said the words in a tired way that suggested he'd spoken them a thousand times. "Ma'am, I need your ID please."

Looking at the small man, Kate handed him her card and asked suspiciously, "Are there any reported incidents of side effects or statistics available regarding accidents with these portals?"

The man gave her a weary look, "Ma'am, they are perfectly safe."

Kate bristled. "Yes, but have there been any lawsuits filed or anything to suggest that others may not share your opinion?"

Tair laughed. "Kate, the only common side effects are extreme fatigue and dizziness by humans when transporting to Shimeria for the first time. On a very rare occasion, a human might faint from the shock to her system, and take longer than usual to recover from the fatigue. However, in your case, it is probable that the portal will faint." His eyes were blatantly teasing.

Kate sniffed. "It was a perfectly legitimate question. I'm merely ascertaining my safety."

The customs official handed back her card. Kate put it in her purse and stepped forward. They were standing now directly in front of the portal. She eyed it suspiciously for a moment. Then, she shot an indignant look at Tair and pronounced, "And I never faint."

She was adorable. Tair laughed. 'I believe you. Really." He knew his voice said just the opposite. He tried to look properly somber, but it was hard with her fairly bristling and vibrating with nerves and indignation.

He attempted a solemn tone. "You must go through the portal alone to signify your free will. Would you like to go first or should I?"

Kate gave him a fuming glance. "I believe you should go first in case of malfunction. If the machine breaks down and transforms your energy into its natural reptilian state as you die a slow horrible death, I would like to be a live witness."

Tair threw back his head and laughed, then leaned down and planted a firm kiss on her mouth. With absolute enjoyment, he said, "Kate, I will be there to greet you in Shimeria. You must step through the portal to see my natural state. I will enjoy showing it to you many, many times. " With another laughing glance, he stepped through the portal.

Kate watched as he disappeared into the blackness and was gone instantly. She stared for a few seconds, and tried to work up her nerve. She would be fine. In spite of his tremendous defects, the intergalactic jerk would never harm her.

The portal was safe. Hell, Sharon and Liken had been through it more than once. Squaring her shoulders, she took a deep breath. Muttering, "My luck I'll be the first reported death," she stepped into the blackness.

Immediately, she was surrounded by dense, crushing blackness. Her lungs seized and she couldn't breath. She lost all orientation. Then, she had a sense of falling and a sudden blinding bright light.

Abruptly Tair's arms wrapped around her and she stood on Shimeria. She looked up to find Tair regarding her with undisguised concern. She said triumphantly, "I told you that I never faint," and promptly passed out cold in his arms.

Chapter 5

She was lying on something cool and slippery. Kate's mind began functioning and memory returned. She opened her eyes slowly, and saw a light green ceiling. As she became aware of a large body beside her, she said, "I did *not* faint."

She was lying in some sort of bed, with dark green, satin-like sheets. In addition, she was suffering from a complete absence of clothing except for said sheet barely covering her upper and lower extremities. She reviewed the known facts. She was here. On another planet. In Bed. Under a sheet. Naked. With an alien. Who was most probably naked, too.

Turning her head slowly to the left, she saw Tair. He was lying on his side, just a little further up in the bed, his head propped in his hand as he watched her. His sculpted, muscular chest was completely bare.

Taking a minute to appreciate the sight, Kate studied the hard contours and the smattering of dark hair. Allowing her gaze to drift downward, she saw that his hips and lower body were covered by the sheet. Barely. She gulped, going cold and then hot. Lifting her eyes to his face, she saw him regarding her with lazy amusement.

Kate closed her eyes and blinked hard, but he was still there. She would not blush. Kate Carson did not blush, *ever*. With studied nonchalance, she grabbed the top of the sheet and pulled it up a little higher and closer to her chest. The movement sent his side of the sheet up a little higher, too. With careful enunciation, she said, "I was suffering from fatigue."

His grin merely widened. "And you fainted."

Kate gave an indignant sniff. "I refuse to descend to the level of childish squabbling. It was not a faint. As I said, I was fatigued."

He laughed and openly teased her. "Of course, how could I assume otherwise? You never faint."

Kate nodded firmly. "Precisely."

Tair said mock solemnly, "Until yesterday."

Kate nearly sat up in surprise and then remembered their nudity. Slumping back down quickly, she exclaimed, "Yesterday? What time is it now?"

Tair reached out slowly and pushed her hair off of her face. "It is evening. You slept all last eve and today. I grew concerned and consulted a healer, but she advised that you would be fine. You merely needed to rest. Earth time and Shimerian time are roughly the same, although you lose a few hours in transition through the portal."

At his tender touch and caring tone, she froze. Men were not tender with her, or at least no one other than Gage. She was used to hot, sweaty bouts of sex followed by quick departures. Hair sweeping, and cuddling and tender touches were not for her. Feeling uncomfortable, she said, "I need a shower. You have facilities here I presume?"

Tair nodded and said softly, "Down the hallway to your left." He waited to see what her next move would be.

Kate thought of her options. She could get up and walk out of the room naked. She was a sexually confident woman with a decent body. She might need to lose a pound or two here or there, but there was no reason for embarrassment. Okay, maybe ten or fifteen pounds, but still she was a sophisticated woman of the world. Or rather, woman of two worlds. She could do it.

Then again, she could take the sheet, wrap it around her and leave *him* naked. Now that particular option sounded like a much better plan.

With sudden boldness, she sat up, pulled the sheet briskly to her and scooted to the edge of the bed. She knew she was flashing him her butt, but it couldn't be helped. Standing up quickly, she wrapped the sheet around her, flinging one end over her shoulder in a particularly stylish move. Holding her head high, she turned around and then stared down at him.

He hadn't moved a muscle in response. Well, a part of him was moving and growing under her gaze. Like some gorgeous statue or painting he was reclining on the bed at perfect ease. His cock hardened as she watched, growing longer and thicker, reaching upward along the muscles of his abdomen until it was about eight inches long.

She could imagine what it would feel like filling and stroking her. She was wet and swollen within seconds, aching for the sensation. Her mouth went dry. Finally, she tore her gaze away and looked at his face. His eyes were heavy-lidded now, and looked dark with arousal. He was no longer smiling.

In a cool tone at odds with the heat in his eyes, he ordered, "Remove the sheet."

The muscles in her thighs tightened. She said in the same tone, "Why should I?"

His mouth took on a cruel edge. He said calmly, "I believe the Challenge Oath involves your compliance with whatever sexual acts I choose to impose."

Kate felt like she was burning up under the heat of his gaze. His eyes were roaming over her with a thoroughness that made the sheet seem superfluous. Her nipples hardened and she knew he could see them pressing outward under the thin confines of the sheet. The satiny material felt cool against her hot skin. The silky feeling against her sensitive nipples was almost too much.

She fought to slow her breathing. An Oath was an Oath. With a calmness she didn't feel, she said, "Fine."

Battling twin urges to leave the sheet on and take it off, she gathered her nerve. If he thought he could best her, he was in for a surprise. Taking the end of the sheet off her shoulder, she pulled it down and began to unwind it with sensual precision.

Drawing out the moment, she took great care to make sure it was a very slow, sexy process. Finally, she dropped the sheet to the floor and stood naked in front of him. Raising her arms upward, she moved her hair back over her shoulders until there was absolutely nothing to impede his view. She brought her hands back down to her sides. Then, she stood there silently, waiting.

Tair was dying by inches. With her hair streaming down and her eyes flashing, she looked like an angry angel he'd seen in a hologram of an Earth painting. The resemblance stopped there. Her breasts were full, the nipples tight and pink and distended. Her waist tapered outward to full hips and long, shapely legs.

There was a triangle of blonde curls covering her sex. He wanted to taste every inch of her, starting right there. His cock ached with the need to plunge into her. He ordered roughly, "Come here."

Kate felt a tremor run through her. He looked so aggressively male, powerful and on the edge of control. She took a few steps forward, very conscious of the sway in her walk as his eyes roamed over her body. Stopping at the edge of the bed, she waited.

Tair smiled, although it looked pained. Sitting up, he scooted his large body to the edge of the bed and put his feet on the floor. They were within inches of each other. Reaching upward, he traced one finger over the upper curve of her breast as he spoke. "When you come, I am going to merge with you. Do you understand what I mean?"

The rough feel of his finger tracing circles on her breast distracted her. Chill bumps followed in its wake. She held her breath, aching for him to touch her nipple. Then, she concentrated hard and reviewed his words. Letting out a breath, she said softly, "We're not having intercourse."

His finger circled around her nipple. His other hand came up and he began tracing with that one, too, on her other breast.

He watched with seemingly total absorption as he said, "I meant I will mind merge with you. It will be slightly painful, but if you relax, you will find the rewards are great."

His fingers moved and she felt twin tugs on her nipples. As he twisted and pulled gently, she stifled a moan. At the muted sound, he looked up. She shook her head no.

His mouth lifted at the corner in a half-smile. "Believe me, *sheka*, you will be willing at the time. I am only telling you now so that you will understand when it happens."

He cupped one swollen breast in his hand. Leaning forward, he licked around and around her aching nipple. The wet feel of his tongue was exquisite. Then, he opened his mouth and sucked.

She groaned and grabbed his head, holding him in place. As he sucked, she panted, "That feels so good. Don't stop."

He obliged her for endless moments before kissing his way over to her other breast. As he licked, nibbled, and sucked, she nearly cried out. Her sex clenched and she ached with a vengeance. She wanted to feel him inside her, pumping in and out. Shutting the temptation out of her mind, she focused on keeping some semblance of control.

He moved one hand down low on her stomach until he reached the top of her curls. Stopping there, he took one nipple in his mouth and bit down with exquisite care. At the tiny pain, Kate's legs began to shake.

When he pulled back, her hands dropped back to her sides. Her arms felt heavy and useless, as if they didn't belong to her.

His hand above her curls moved around to her side, and then back to cup one hip. His other hand moved to do the same. He held her gaze as he asked, "Are you wet, Kate?" His tone said he knew she was beyond wet.

Kate complied as he pushed her backward a step and then kneeled on the floor, still holding her hips. Her stomach muscles tightened as he leaned forward. Kate licked her dry lips, and watched as he placed gentle kisses low on her stomach. The hands holding her hips flexed and relaxed in a rhythm that reminded her forcibly of the pleasures of having him inside her, stroking in that same way. Feeling like she was drowning, she gasped out, "You know I am."

He looked up at her with hungry eyes and muttered, "Not enough" against the top of her curls. Pulling her forward, he moved his head downward and pressed a gentle kiss to her clitoris. Kate froze. For an endless moment he did nothing else.

Then, she felt the moist heat of his tongue as he circled her clit. She moaned and leaned forward, shaking with need. He lapped at her with obvious enjoyment, moving down to her opening and then back up to her clit. As he circled and sucked gently, she shuddered and moaned. Her legs gave out, but she felt him strengthen his hold and take more of her weight to keep her standing.

Suddenly he stopped and stood, abruptly lifting her in his arms. Kate felt her heart skip a beat as he placed her on the bed, then crawled between her legs and pushed them apart with firm hands. When his mouth returned to her aching sex, she fell backward and arched up into his mouth.

Kate shuddered as he responded with firmer pressure and the thrust of one long finger inside of her. She was on the edge of control, but fighting to remain level-headed. They couldn't have intercourse, no matter how much she wanted him. She was not staying on Shimeria with him, she reminded herself grimly. She had no sooner finished that thought when she felt Tair thrust a second finger inside her and begin moving both fingers in and out. Her mind shut down.

After long moments of delicious torture, she was actively thrusting up against his mouth, only to feel him lift his head. She looked down at him in agonized disbelief.

Maintaining the motions of his fingers, Tair said roughly, "I could put my cock in you now. Imagine how it will feel as I pump into you. Say yes, and let me fill you."

Kate shook her head from side to side in a motion of denial. Her whole body was flushed and shaking as if she had a fever. She couldn't form any words of reply.

Tair muttered something that sounded suspiciously like a curse word. In a husky voice, he asked, "Do you want to come?"

Kate found her voice, but it was unsteady. "Yes." She felt her lower body clench. She had to come soon. The need was killing her.

Tair said bluntly, "We will merge when you come. Do you still want it?"

Kate closed her eyes, in agony. She had never wanted anything more in her life than an orgasm at that moment. Merging was only some mind thing. How bad could it be? With a groan of frustration, she said, "Yes."

Tair heard the word with a sense of triumph. He sucked on her clit and entered her mind in one strong thrust. He groaned in reaction to the sensation of joining with Kate, of really knowing her, and held onto control with sheer will. He had to be careful not to hurt her too much.

A stabbing pain shot through her head. Kate cried out as tears sprang to her eyes. Her hands moved reflexively to her head. She could feel Tair move through her mind in one long slow wave.

Suddenly, she felt his arousal and pleasure pouring into her. He stabbed at her clit with his tongue, pressing upward in her sex with his fingers as if he knew exactly how it felt. As she moaned and tensed, she was overwhelmed at the pleasure building back and forth between them. The mixture of his pleasure and her own sent her over the edge. Arching, she screamed hoarsely and felt her sex pulse as wave after wave of intense pleasure went through her. She went rigid and then collapsed with relief.

As the waves gradually died, she felt Tair finally lift his head. She was too relaxed to move, so she lay there staring at the ceiling. She would deal with what had happened in a minute or maybe an hour. She would be Killer Kate Carson in a minute. Right now, she was content to be an amoeba.

Tair had found his own release when Kate went over the edge. Their combined pleasure had been too much for his control. He felt as if every drop of energy in his body had been drained. In slow movements, he crawled weakly up beside her. Using his last bit of energy, he turned onto his side and wrapped an arm across her stomach. He waited as they both lay there breathing harshly in the silence of the room.

Kate's brain re-engaged slowly. It wasn't easy with her body still flushed and relaxed, but she knew she needed to concentrate. Sex was not supposed to be so powerful and all-consuming. It was supposed to be pleasurably intense, nothing more. This had been beyond her scope of experience.

She knew she should feel worried, but it was hard when she felt so good. Giving herself a good mental shake, she forced herself to examine the facts. He had merged with her. And she had agreed to it.

With a touch of bite in her voice directed more at herself than at him, she said, "I guess you won this particular battle."

Tair's brain was beginning to function better, too. She had stunned him. He couldn't believe the effect she had on his senses. The taste of her, the feel of her, was incredible. She could set him on fire with a mere look. Seeing her so totally lost to his touch had moved him emotionally, too.

Being so far inside her mind had been unbelievably pleasurable. Her inner beauty was an incredible wonder. The ache to claim her body was like a living thing inside him. He was not pleased to be so intensely affected. With a self-derisive smile, he said, "I am not sure either of us won."

Kate moved her head to look at him. She would have thought he would be crowing and acting impossibly arrogant by now. She studied him in silence for a moment and then asked, "What do you mean?"

Tair looked away from her thoughtful gaze and stared at the wall. In a self-mocking voice, he said, "Kate, I am not interested in anything beyond friendship and great sex. I will cherish you as my pactmate and then as my pledgemate, but I do not want to fall in love with anyone, including you. Ever."

Fragile hope, newly born and unspoken even to herself, died swiftly at his words. Of course, he didn't want to love her. She didn't want to love him either. The whole idea was preposterous.

With chilly emphasis she said, "I don't recall asking for your love. I was merely referring to the merge. It seems to me you're too familiar with clinging, brainless females. I have no interest in anything beyond a brief two-week affair. We can have sexual fun without intercourse and without emotion. You're the one you who brought up infantile emotions like love."

Her eyes were ice cold and her body was rigid beneath his arm. Tair felt his own heart clutch as the hurt his words caused passed over him. He gave a mental sigh and wondered how to explain without doing further damage.

He felt uncomfortable and unsure how to proceed. Searching for words, he said, "I meant I did not expect to feel so intensely affected by you. It is not of my choosing."

Kate felt her heart lodge in her throat. A feeling of warmth surged that had nothing to do with desire. This emotional stuff was too much on her nerves. She did not believe in morning-after drama or weird pillow talk. She felt uncomfortable and out of her depth. She sat up, pushing his arm away abruptly, and moved up and off the bed quickly.

Standing two feet from the bed looking down at him, she crossed her arms over her chest. In icy tones, she said, "This conversation is officially over. I am not up to emotional pillow talk. You're male. You should be snoring by now. What's wrong with you?"

He propped his head in his hand and gave a mock sigh. "I believe *you* are what is wrong with me, *sheka*."

Kate said tartly, "Then get over it. This nonsense is ridiculous. Get some sleep because when I get back from my shower, we're going to discuss this merging business. Believe me, you want to rest up."

He laughed and watched her as she turned to stare at each wall of the room. There was truly no one like her on this world or any other. He waited patiently.

Kate looked from wall to wall but there was no doorway. It made no sense. How did the two of them get in? What kind of whacked out Harry Houdini world was this anyway? With an exasperated sigh, she demanded, "Tell me how to get out."

He tried to keep a straight face, but it wasn't easy. In a serious tone, he said, "It is the wall directly across from you. Press the button on the right side and the wall slides to form a doorway."

She muttered an icy, "Thank you," and stepped forward. Pressing the button, she watched as the wall slid open upon itself, making a hole like a doorway. With as much dignified grace as she could manage while naked and feeling like an idiot, she walked through it and down the hall.

Tair remained there grinning, wondering what she would think of a Shimerian shower. Her reactions and observations never failed to entertain him. With a muffled laugh he settled back and waited to find out.

Kate saw a button on the left wall of the hallway and pressed it. Once again, the wall opened. She peered in cautiously and discovered a fairly ordinary bathroom.

There was no mirror, but the toilet looked pretty much like any toilet on Earth. The lid was down. Now that truly was amazing. A man who not only remembered to flip the seat down but closed the lid as well.

Suddenly, the door slid closed behind her. She heard a small squeak at the same time. She didn't bother to turn around. The door must have a sensor or a timer. Stepping further into the room, she spotted the shower stall in the far corner. She walked to it and saw a single lever. Now that was weird. Grimacing with distaste, she hoped it was not ice-cold water she'd be feeling.

She stuck her arm under it while pulling the lever downward. Blood gushed from the showerhead and poured over her hand like a warm waterfall. Horrified, Kate felt her knees go weak and her stomach clutch.

With a small moan, she stepped backward, only to feel something alive and wriggling under her foot. She screamed and jumped forward toward the stall. The blood continued to spew. Desperate to look somewhere, anywhere else, she glanced down and froze.

Right by her foot, she saw a creature that looked like a large rat with huge ears and a furry striped tail. It was hissing at her and baring long pointy teeth. Its eyes bulged and its back arched, poised to attack. Still screaming, she felt her vision gray. The last thing she saw was the creature fall over on its side with a thump.

Chapter 6

Tair heard her scream and sprang from the bed. Opening the wall, he ran through it and down the hallway with his heart in his throat. Had she fallen? Was she injured? He could no longer feel her. He opened the wall to the bathroom, crying out her name frantically, "Kate!"

He stopped abruptly in the doorway. Both Kate and his pet, Deva, were lying on the floor with the shower running. Rushing to Kate, he quickly squatted and touched her face. He asked urgently, "Kate, are you alright?"

When she opened her eyes, he scanned her thoughts and sank down on the floor in relief. With a shaky hand, he ran his hand through his hair. Then he raked his hands over his face. Finally, he dropped his head into his hands.

A minute went by. Eventually raising his head, he said, "Kate, we must talk about your habit of *not* fainting. My heart cannot take the strain."

Kate sat up slowly. He reached forward suddenly and wrapped her tightly in his arms. She could feel his heart beating like a drum against her chest.

She leaned against him weakly and took deep breaths. Hearing the sound of running liquid, she shuddered and said faintly, "Please. Turn it off."

Immediately, the shower stopped. Kate tried to regain her composure but it was proving nearly impossible. She felt sick and shaky, but there was something happening that was causing her worse distress. Tair's emotions were bombarding her in rapid succession: fear, relief, and exasperation were all flooding into her at an alarming rate.

She was not about to discuss how she could feel his emotions right now. Not to mention how he had stopped that hellish shower. She said in a stronger voice, "Thank you. And I will thank you even more if you refrain from telling me how you did it. I'm sure it involves superhero powers I'd just as soon not confront at the moment." She pulled away from him and sat up straight.

He nodded and leaned back against the wall. Kate remained sitting, looking at his gray face. Okay, so she'd freaked out a little. So she had a rather strong reaction to the sight of blood. They both needed to get a grip on their messy emotions. Lifting her chin, she demanded, "What the hell kind of vampire wet dream was that?"

Tair gave her an exasperated look and said distinctly, "Kate, the dark red liquid is *vara*. It is similar to your water. And it is absolutely, definitely, beyond any doubt *not* blood of any kind."

Feeling foolish, she went on the defensive immediately. "And I was supposed to know that *how*?"

Remembering the attacking rat-thing suddenly, she looked around frantically. Spotting it on its side apparently dead, near the wall, she scooted back to Tair's side of the room and leaned against the wall next to him.

With pure revulsion, she asked, "And another thing...What the hell is that? Don't you have any kind of pest control here?"

Tair's mouth lifted at the corners in the beginnings of a grin. "*That* is Deva, and although she is a pest, she is also my pet." His smile grew wider as he saw Kate's incredulous face.

Kate couldn't believe it. She didn't bother hiding her disgust. "You keep a rat for a pet?"

Tair laughed. He couldn't help it. His shoulders shook and it was some time before he could choke out, "No."

Kate watched him laugh like a loon and wondered what kind of idiot person would keep a big ugly rat as a pet. Not her kind of person. *Yuck.* With an arched brow, she waited impatiently for an explanation.

Tair brought his laughter under control finally. With sparkling eyes, he said, "Deva is not a rat. Deva is a *sheka*."

There were pet names and then there were pet names. Kate felt her temper engage and grow with astronomic speed. In clipped accents, she said, "As an endearment, you refer to me as a rat?!"

Seeing the anger in her flashing eyes, Tair felt a tug of answering desire. She looked beautiful and deadly, but he supposed he should try to calm her. Crawling across the floor, he picked up Deva carefully and began stroking her stomach. With a quiet purr, Deva shapeshifted back into her natural form.

Kate watched as Tair picked up the dead rat thing. Turning it over onto its back, he rubbed its stomach gently. The thing purred and then changed into a furry creature with sad brown eyes. It seemed to peer at her with hurt accusation.

It looked kind of like a kitten only with the longer nose and floppy ears of a dog. It had large whiskers and a shiny brown coat that looked soft. She blinked, but the cat/dog was still there and the rat was nowhere in sight. Taking a deep breath, she let it out slowly.

Tair rubbed Deva along her back and explained to Kate. "*Shekas* are very affectionate, loyal, loveable creatures. They only look so fierce when something scares them." He gave her a long look.

Kate gave him a defiant glare in response, including the rat-cat-dog for good measure. "How does it change? I thought it was dead."

Tair shook his head and put Deva down on the floor. Still petting her, he said, "They are what you would call shapeshifters. They are common here. Generally, they shift as a defense mechanism to scare their attackers. If the situation appears life-threatening, they will fall over and play dead. It tends to confuse predators. You must have scared her badly."

Kate said indignantly, "Oh, I like that. *I* scared *her* badly. What about me? Between her and the gushing blood I..."

Tair shot her a big grin and arched an eyebrow as he waited.

Kate changed words and said calmly, "...collapsed with fatigue."

Tair appeared to give her words some thought, very seriously. Then he said teasingly, "Now that I consider it, my choice of endearment is even more appropriate. You and Deva were both on the floor *collapsed with fatigue* when I arrived."

Kate sniffed and said primly, "Are we through with the annoying banter? I came in here for a reason. Your absence would be appreciated and highly enjoyed."

She moved and stood up gingerly. Her legs were shaky and she felt exhausted. This planet was not exactly a traveler's dream. It was confusing and weird. She needed a shower and she needed to go to sleep again.

Tair said gently, "Kate, Shimeria holds many wonders. Please do not judge too quickly."

She knew the blood was draining from her face. In a shaky voice, she demanded, "Tell me you did not just read my mind."

Tair winced at the unsteadiness of her voice. She had been pushed far enough. There was plenty of time for explanations later. In a careful voice, he said, "Under these circumstances, your thoughts are easily guessed."

Kate sensed an evasion somewhere but was too tired to protest or pursue it. With steadier legs, she moved toward the shower. As she walked, she ordered crisply, "Please leave. And take your little rat-dog, too."

He could always return, he reminded himself. He would know if she felt unwell again. She needed time alone. Tair picked up Deva and walked out of the bathroom. Heading down the hall, he put Deva in the kitchen next to her food, and then walked back to the bedroom. Lying down on the bed, he waited for Kate to return.

* * * * *

Kate leaned against the stall wall in the bathroom, with the warm *vara* washing over her body. Now that she was under it, she wondered how she could have ever mistaken it for blood. It was strangely slick and it felt amazingly refreshing. The liquid didn't cling to her skin. Instead it flowed over her body, leaving her feeling clean and dry almost as soon as she stepped out from under it. She moved away from the wall again and marveled anew at the sensation of being dry almost at once.

She chided herself inwardly for her foolishness. She had overreacted. The shower was not a nightmare but a pleasure. She was suffering from a combination of excessive emotion and exhaustion. Her wits had taken a vacation since she stepped through that portal. In the morning, she was going to take charge once and for all.

Later, slipping into the bed in the darkened bedroom, she pulled up the covers and stared into blackness. Tair rolled toward her and wrapped his arm around her, bringing his whole body against hers, spooning. She went rigid in protest and muttered, "Get off me, will you?"

There was no answer from him. He continued to hold her. After a full minute, she gave up, sighed, and enjoyed the warmth of his body against her back. Tomorrow, she would fight him. She would be back to her old self. And she would win.

Tair tightened his arm in response to her thought. In a soft voice, he said, "Go to sleep, Kate."

Kate gave a weary sigh, feeling too tired to fight him and her own body's need for sleep. She would win tomorrow, no doubt about it. She gave in and drifted off to sleep.

Tair lay there in the darkness, feeling restless and aroused at the weight of her soft body against his own. This pact business was getting complicated. It should have been simple--claim his pactmate, play an enjoyable sexual game to win her, and then settle into a comfortable, affectionate existence. Challenge her, seduce her, pledge her, and keep her. A neat, orderly, plan without strong, messy emotions clouding the issue. However, Kate was making things difficult.

She would not be pleased to learn he could read her mind at any time. She would be even less pleased with some of the other things awaiting her. His last thought before he drifted off to sleep was the image of Kate climaxing against his mouth. She was going to fight him every step of the way. But he would win in the end.

Chapter 7

Tair came awake slowly, aware suddenly of an absence in the bed. Kate was nowhere to be seen. He felt an immediate desire to find her and enact a passionate repeat of last night. His mind filled with images of how she'd looked, arching upward against his mouth, lost completely in pleasure.

As his cock, already hard, throbbed in response, Tair reached out telepathically to read Kate. The answering response he received was so mentally loud, his hands went to his head instinctively and he winced.

"I know you are awake in there, thanks to this wretched merging! Come and face me you horny, low-life, despicable, morally-bankrupt louse of an alien!" Her words were shouted mentally and the anger behind them gave them real telepathic strength.

Tair sighed. Throwing up a mental block to shut her out, he pondered the best course of action. Kate was awake and ready and he was still cloudy with sleep. He had barely slept last eve, restlessly waking and wanting her.

She had felt so warm and sweetly desirable, sleepily cuddling in his arms. Grimacing, he wondered if she would ever be that defenselessly sweet while actually conscious. Determined to let her rest, he had been careful not to wake her or make any demands.

Thinking about it now, he wondered if the restraint had been a good idea. She was refreshed and determined and he was barely functioning. Getting out of bed, he headed to the bathroom. He would face her when he was awake and showered.

No male could be expected to deal well with a female in full fury – especially an unpredictable Earth female -- without some preparation. With Kate, being less than awake would be a major mistake. Feeling misused and grumpy, he wondered what had led to her mood. Earth females were entirely too emotional. He stood under the shower and leaned blearily into the *vara*.

Kate needed to understand that she was not the one in control. Whatever it was that had led to her fury, he decided he would learn soon enough. And deal with it...when he was awake...in just another moment...or two...or ten...

* * * * *

Kate felt his mental withdrawal with profound relief. Concentrating and mentally screaming at him had been a calculated risk. As she heard the shower running, her shoulders relaxed. She had a little more time to plan. Looking at the screen in front of her, she continued to jot down notes.

Twenty minutes later, refreshed, grimly ready for battle, and fully alert, Tair stood in the archway and peered cautiously in the kitchen. Kate had her hair tied back in an Earth-style knot and was wearing some of the Shimerian garments from the sleeping chamber closet. There was a flush on her cheekbones, but her face was otherwise pale. Her lips, in major contrast, were painted a deep, dramatic red.

She looked beautiful and passionately intense. She was sitting at the table using her personal tech unit. As she scribbled with the stylus on the small screen in front of her, he wondered if he should try to scan her before she was on her guard again. Kate looked up and the opportunity passed.

Kate felt her breath catch at the sight of Tair in the doorway. His hair was a little curlier from his shower and he was dressed in a black shirt and black pants. He was barefoot and leaning casually in the archway watching her.

The look in his eyes was completely intimate, and intensely male, as if he was recalling her body in vivid detail. She remembered what had happened the previous night between them and felt warm desire flood her. Her nipples tightened in response.

Suddenly worried that he would read her thoughts, she demanded flatly, "I want your oath that you'll stay out of my head for this discussion."

Tair thought about it for a moment. He asked curiously, "Why should I do as you ask?"

Kate lifted her chin. With cool precision, she said, "Because if you don't, I'm going to scream at you mentally, and I mean constantly. I will give you the worst headache known to science. And you will have gained nothing. Your choice."

Tair considered her words. She would do it. What she didn't realize was that he was an expert prober. Eventually, he could get past her surface thoughts and seek the information he wanted. He had done it many times with criminals in his capacity as a Guardian.

However, it might be easier to do as she requested. It would spare both of them a headache. He would appear to be acting very reasonably and making an effort to accommodate her. It was a small concession with potential rewards.

Nodding his head, he said lightly, "Upon my oath I will not scan your thoughts while we have this conversation. However, after this conversation, I promise nothing."

Kate felt triumph flood her. She was over the first hurdle and it had been a big one. Gesturing at the chair across the table from her, she said, "Okay, then. Why don't you take a seat and we'll get started."

She was trying to control the situation from the beginning. He knew what she was doing and was not in the least surprised. Playing along with her for the moment, he strode across the room and took a seat. Reaching out and grabbing a *nidsu* from the bowl on the table, he bit into it with a loud crunch.

Kate watched him warily. Chewing it slowly, he swallowed, and then said casually, "I believe you have been quite busy. I see you have managed to find firstmeal and are working already. Was your tech unit in your purse?"

Ignoring the way his tongue came out to get the juice from the fruit off his upper lip, she kept her attention on his eyes. It wasn't easy. With a brisk nod, she said, "Yes, I had it in my purse. I wasn't about to leave it on Earth. It's very useful for organization."

Tair nodded in agreement. He knew of her fondness for organization already. He was merely easing into the situation cautiously. Leaning back in his chair, he asked, "You *have* eaten?"

It was time to go to war. Kate said flatly, "Yes, I've eaten. I've explored the house, pushed nearly every button, and learned quite a few things."

Tair had a sudden sinking feeling. She had been up for quite some time, obviously. He needed to assess the damage. "How long have you been awake?"

Kate gave him her best glacial smile. "Long enough. About three hours. "Giving him a significant look, she added, "I am no longer fatigued."

Tair winced mentally. Three hours, it was too long. With studied indifference, he asked, "I suppose you found our home computer?"

Kate's smile widened. Oh boy, had she found the computer. And what an informative session it had been. She said somewhat smugly, "Why, yes I did. I even realized fairly quickly how to request the English translation. You *are* very good with preparations and details."

The situation was getting worse by the moment. Tair felt a sense of dread. She had found the culture tutorial. He knew it. Arching an eyebrow he asked, "And the security password?"

Kate remembered that moment of triumph and flashed him a triumphant look. "It was easy to surmise that my ID card went into the slot. It turned on and gave me a blank screen."

She sat back in her chair. "Then, I tried typing 'Tair', 'Liken', 'Sharon', 'Jadik', 'Kate', and *sheka*'. I had almost given up. "

"Then, I typed 'Deva' and I was in." Her smile was all teeth and she knew it. She could almost forgive the little rat for scaring the hell out of her last night in light of her triumph this morning.

Tair cursed mentally. He knew it was poor security to use a pet's name as a password, but he had been thinking at the time of making it easier for Kate to remember. He had planned to show her the computer, and at the appropriate time, he would have shown her the cultural tutorial to help her better understand her new home. But she had accessed it now.

He had to know. The time for game-playing was done. With simple directness, he said, "You accessed 'sexual practices'."

Kate knew her anger was clear on her face. She had been curious about quite a few things, and that one had been near the top. However, she hadn't needed to type in "sexual practices."

She stared at him. "No, actually I was looking at mental abilities when I saw a reference to linking." Remembering with fresh horror what the tutorial said, she stated with arctic, final emphasis, "I will not link with Jadik or anyone else."

Tair sighed in frustration. Earth females were so impossible when it came to this subject. Sharon had been very difficult about it, too. He did not understand why it was so upsetting. It was perfectly natural and expected. It was Shimerian law, and a time-honored and important part of their culture. Why did Earth females react so violently to the idea? It was no wonder that Shimerians made sure it was kept a secret from humans. Scrubbing a hand over his face, he said, "I knew you would react in this way."

Kate remembered the cold weight that had settled over her when she read about linking. Human females were completely defenseless against mind rape by a Shimerian. With merging, apparently Tair had placed a mental shield around her mind. Theoretically, the Shimerian pactmate chose a male friend or relative to "link" with his mate. The 'link' used his mental power to add an additional mental shield to protect the female.

In addition, the link had a "connection," like a door, that could be opened at will. The door was really a small barrier that would be breeched instantly if the female became severely distressed. In times of great emotion, the female would be more or less "shouting" and the link would mentally hear. It was for the protection of the female.

Linking was not required only of human females either. Even Shimerian females each had a link. Shimerian females had a natural mental shield. However, in a society that treasured and protected females, having a pactmate and a link was a way to ensure the highest protection. Essentially, two male protectors were considered better than one.

The problem was that the "linking" was done at the female's point of orgasm, when her mental defenses were completely down. Basically, there was a sexual threesome "linking ceremony." That Tair would even consider sharing her with someone else was insulting. It proved quite effectively that he did not care for her in the least.

She was fine with the notion. If a part of her was cold and empty at the thought, it was merely a leftover sense of emotionalism from the intensity of last night. She didn't care what the tutorial for Planet Kink explained. She was not participating in a threesome. And Tair was a louse.

Tair watched the emotions play over Kate's face. She was hurt under all that anger. He knew it, but had no idea how to sooth her. With a great deal more sympathy for Liken's struggle with Sharon over the topic, he tried to find the words to make her understand.

He began in a gentle voice. "I have no desire to share you with another. Linking is a very natural thing. It is a ceremony of great tradition and honor. Your protection is my uppermost importance. The sexuality of it is a harmless thing. It only occurs once."

Kate raised a skeptical eyebrow. She said sarcastically, "Let me make sure I understand. You and I have sex with Jadik, but it's harmless. And, oh, yes, it's all for my benefit."

Tair placed both hands on the table and leaned forward earnestly, "Kate, you and I will make love, with Jadik there in the same room. At the point of your orgasm, I will work to lower the shield I have put in place around your mind. Jadik will work to build a pathway from his mind to yours and place his shield over mine. As your link, he needs a way to receive your thoughts if you are in distress."

Kate rubbed her neck absently in an attempt to ease the ache. He was saying pretty much what the information on the computer had said. The "link" was a kind of backup if the pactmate was injured, dead, or unable to aid in the even of an emergency to the female.

She was smart enough to understand rationally that she was on a different planet and the culture was very different. It didn't make it any easier for her to understand from her own cultural point of view. She could see the sincerity in Tair. He truly did not believe there was anything wrong with linking.

It was confusing to her emotionally. Uncomfortable with the sensation, she said coolly, "I understand it's to keep criminals from attempting some kind of mind rape. As a human, I'm especially vulnerable without any natural shields."

"Now that we're merged..." She gave him a killing look. "...I have a single shield that could still be breeched. Unlike before, however, the amount of power needed to rip through that shield would do a lot of damage. A second shield is greater protection."

She rubbed her forehead wearily. She should never have agreed to a merge. She had heard rumors of telepathic powers, but had not considered the full implications. What a big miscalculation on her part it had been to assume it was temporary -- an extra sense that came into play during sex.

The merge was permanent. She'd like to blame Tair for not telling her, but she had not even asked. It was her own fault for allowing it. When she had realized that this morning, her sense of horror had been overwhelming. She had him stuck in her head now. He could withdraw and block her at times, but he would be there always. There was no going back.

Well, what was done was done. No matter how she hated it, there was no changing it. "I'll concede it makes sense. But I don't like the thought of you running around in my head, much less someone else I don't even know."

Tair felt his shoulders relax. She was trying to understand. It was a start. He thought carefully how to phrase his next point.

In the same earnest tone, he said, "Kate, Jadik is completely trustworthy. He would give his life to protect you. I trust him with my life, with both our lives. He will not intrude on your privacy without good reason. He is my best friend. Other than my brother, there is no one I trust more. That trust is very important when it comes to the shielding process."

He ran his hand through his hair in frustration. "I do not know how to make you understand."

He reached across the table and gathered one of her hands in his own. "The sexuality of it is completely natural and depends upon the three participants. It will go only as far as the three of us decide it will go. He will need to be there and the less clothing and the more intimacy between the two of you, the easier it is to link. However, it will be done with your full consent. You have nothing to fear."

Kate swallowed past the huge lump in her throat. He made it all sound so reasonable. In spite of her misgivings she felt a lurking arousal at the thought of a linking ceremony between the three of them. A picture of Jadik flashed into her head, beautiful and dangerous. It scared the hell out of her.

Tair could see the sudden darkening of her eyes and guess at her thoughts. He said softly, "I have been inside your mind. The thought of linking should not be completely abhorrent. You are attracted to Jadik."

Before she could stop herself, Kate asked, "Doesn't that bother you?"

Tair looked surprised at the notion. "No. Attraction is a natural thing between two adults. It is not the same as what is between us. You are my pactmate and you will be my pledgemate."

He could see she did not understand. He tried to think of it in terms of her culture. "In your culture, the sexuality of the linking would be like harmless flirting. It means nothing. Perhaps the equivalent of when various males kiss the bride at her wedding. It is considered fun and harmless, not a threatening or insulting thing."

A sudden thought occurred to her. "Sharon did this?! I can't believe it. You're her link?"

Tair smiled. "Yes, I am her link."

Kate wasn't sure how she felt about it. This was all so weird. The thought of Sharon and Tair... She felt a little tug of jealousy. "The three of you..."

Tair raised an eyebrow, although he could not help being pleased at the flash of jealousy that had been obvious. He asked calmly, "Yes?"

Kate knew she shouldn't ask, but she had to know. "Did you have sex with her?"

Tair asked, "Why should it matter? You and I had taken no oaths with each other at the time."

Kate felt angry at the evasion. "Just tell me."

He leaned back in the chair. "What happens at the ceremony is usually kept between the participants. However, I will be honest and tell you that I did not have sex with her. Only kissing and some touching were involved. Beyond that, I will not share details."

Kate felt a sense of relief. It shouldn't matter, but it did. She knew how much Liken and Sharon loved each other. It was obvious to her, too, that Tair and Sharon had a warm affection between them, nothing more. Still, she felt better knowing they hadn't slept together.

Tair broke her thoughts. "Kate, linking is perfectly natural and harmless. It is necessary for protection and it is an important part of our culture. Because it is different from your own culture does not mean it is wrong."

He made a certain bizarre sense from an intellectual standpoint. It was a cultural difference, but she could understand the reasoning. Unfortunately, she couldn't shake her discomfort. She and Tair and Jadik... She wasn't Shimerian and she wasn't raised to believe this kind of stuff. She felt confused and scared. She hated feeling this way. It really pissed her off.

She said flatly, "I don't care if you've been training to focus and search for a pactmate telepathically your whole life. I don't believe this idiotic destined mate business. It's just a way to convince women to stay."

Tair watched the ice return to Kate's expression and knew he had pushed her far enough for the moment. She was highly intelligent and would need time to deal with the information. It was time to distract her.

It was time for some fun. Deliberately goading her, he said, "I believe this conversation is over." His voice was a mocking echo of her usual statement.

When her eyes flashed in response, he smiled. "It is time for us to explore your new home."

Giving him a lethal look, she said, "This is not my home. This is my temporary housing unit until I return to my home."

"Not true, *sheka*," he denied, grinning wider.

He added, "However, because I am such a wonderful louse of an alien I am willing to show you Shimeria. Unless your encounters with the portal and Deva have scared you too much to explore."

Kate felt her temper boil, and struggled to control it. He was provoking her on purpose. In a tone of pure ice, she said, "In spite of your pathetically obvious attempt to goad me into doing what you want, I would like to see more of your planet than just this house."

Tair stood up and looked down at her. She raised a resentful eyebrow at his position. His expression changed abruptly to one she recognized instantly. He was about to get sexual and in a big way.

He said in a voice brooking no argument, "I believe it is time for us to establish some rules. When we are alone together in this *temporary housing unit* you will remain nude at all times unless I tell you otherwise. I will touch you with my hands and my mouth any time I desire."

Kate could feel her blood heating at his words. It was infuriating to know that he could get to her with one simple statement. She took a deep breath and opened her mouth to speak.

Tair held his hand up and watched as her mouth closed in response. Good. She was off-balance already. Smiling coolly, he said calmly, "I know your fantasies, Kate. I know what you want and how you want it. It is my goal to give you exactly those things. In return, you will not argue with every sexual order, especially when you know very well you desire it as much as I. You enjoy it when I talk to you in this way. It arouses you. You will enjoy a great many other things as well."

She stood up, thinking frantically. Things were moving fast. She should protest at his high-handed orders, but at the same time he was doing it in response to her own fantasies. It was confusing. Then, grimly, she wondered if he was reading her thoughts.

Tair shrugged. "Yes, I am scanning you. In return for your cooperation, I will give you privacy at certain times. I will try to tell you when I block you, although you will probably be able to feel it."

Searching through her mind, he stopped at one particular idea. With a sudden wide grin, he said, "Kate, how very intriguing. What an interesting fantasy life you have inside that beautiful mind."

Kate could feel his satisfaction and growing desire. Whatever he had found out, he was feeling enthusiastic. Kate Carson did not blush, not ever.

She reminded herself of that fact, even as she felt her face heat. The damn man was so infuriating. Walking past him, she said regally, "If you're reading my mind, you know damn well how I feel about it."

She looked over her shoulder and exclaimed, "Are we going or not?"

Tair made a swift decision. They were going, but not quite yet. He said firmly, "Kate."

She stopped in the archway and turned to face him. With an arched brow and a furious look, she asked, "What now?"

Tair said coolly, "You will precede me to our sleeping chamber. I must retrieve something."

Her heart began beating faster. The bedroom was dangerous territory. Shrugging and acting nonchalant, she said, "Whatever. Let's go." She turned and walked away.

Walking down the hallway, she plotted quickly. She was no coward and she intended to make that point crystal clear. If he wanted to engage in sexual game-playing, she would start the game with a play of her own. Entering the bedroom, she walked straight to the bed and laid down. Rolling until she was on her side facing the doorway, she propped her head in her hand in a familiar pose.

Tair knew what she was doing, but paused in the doorway at the sight of her. She surprised him constantly. There was no one on any planet exactly like Kate. His cock hardened and throbbed with the need to join her on the bed. Feeling his heart rate climb, he worked to appear outwardly composed.

In all his probing of human minds while on vacations on Earth, he had learned an extensive variety and understanding of slang. The expression "hell-on-wheels" had been custom-made for Kate.

Seeing his hardened cock press against the front of his pants, Kate gave him a triumphant smile. In a sultry voice, she challenged, "Well, lover, what exactly did you want to retrieve?"

Tair felt his temperature climb at her husky voice and provocative words. Reminding himself that strategy was important in any challenge, he walked to the wall next to the bed. Pressing a button, he waited as the wall slid open to reveal shelves. Finally, reaching in toward the back, he located what he sought.

Kate watched him in puzzled silence. What was he doing? She hadn't pressed that particular button this morning because of the proximity to the bed.

Seeing him take out an object wrapped in some kind of plastic-like material, she watched as he unwrapped it. Whatever the thing was, it was obviously brand new. He held the object in one hand and the wrapper in another. Then, he stared in concentration at the wrapper a moment. The wrapping material crumpled into smaller and smaller dust and then disappeared.

Kate choked. "Well, that's a new way to take out the trash."

Tair was puzzled for a moment, and then realized what she meant. Smiling, he explained, "The material is made to disintegrate. Anyone with the slightest ability can make it crumble."

Kate said, "Oookay. Good to know."

Tair climbed onto the bed and pushed her gently onto her back, still holding the *mityb* in his right hand. Then, he put the *mityb* on the far corner of the bed. Climbing over her, he pushed one leg between her thighs and pushed them apart. He brought his hard cock between into the cradle of her legs and gave a gentle nudge, keeping most of his weight on his arms.

Kate felt him against her sex and bit her lip from the pleasure that burst through her. She was wet from no more than that one gentle push.

Looking up into his face, she worked to hide the effect. There was something about having a man over you, his cock hard against your sex. It produced an almost primal sense of arousal. It was so unfair.

Tair watched as she bit her lip. Leaning down, he licked the tiny hurt away. Pressing his lips against hers, he began nibbling gently. Against her mouth, between kisses, he said, "Put your arms over your head."

Kate had been on the verge of closing her eyes, but opened them. His lips against hers felt wonderful, although she ached for more. She wanted a deep, hot, wet kiss. Tair's eyes darkened even further and she realized he was still reading her thoughts. Willing to play, she pulled up her arms until they rested over her head.

Tair gave her a harder kiss in reward. Dipping his tongue just inside her lips, he traced and then drew back and planted more tiny kisses against her mouth. Raising back a little, he ordered, "Keep them there."

Kate asked defiantly, "And if I don't?"

Tair said between a new flurry of soft kisses, "You will pay...a penalty. It may not...be something...you would like...to pay at this time."

Kate arched an eyebrow. The feel of his gentle kisses in contrast to the firmness of his words was strangely arousing. Then Tair began kissing her in earnest. His mouth moved with mobile precision, gentle then demanding, until she felt like she would lose her mind.

With a moan, she opened her mouth and began tracing his mouth with her tongue. Suddenly, he thrust his tongue against hers. The kiss turned into a battle to satisfy their hunger. The velvet feel of his tongue against her own excited her and had her craving the act they were imitating.

Abruptly, he broke the kiss and began placing small kisses along her cheek, over to her ear, and then the side of her neck. Biting and sucking, he made the nerves in her neck come to life. He slid down a little and continued until he reached the neckline of her blouse.

He licked a slow line along the edge. She hadn't thought it was possible, but her nipples drew even tighter. She wanted his mouth there, soothing that ache. He lifted up suddenly and rocked back onto his knees. She asked in surprise, "What?"

Tair smiled that infuriating half-smile in response. Then he reached down and ripped her blouse open in one quick motion. Kate was stunned. Leaning back down, he began licking her nipple and then sucking it. Kate shut her eyes at the feel of his mouth on her breast, wet heat against aching tightness.

He moved to the other one, laving and sucking until she arched her back in helpless response. At her movement, he continued with renewed fervor, and then moved downward and placed kisses along her stomach until he reached the waistband of the skirt. It was knee-length, but loose.

Kate wondered if he would pull it up or rip it off. In answer, he moved back and then ripped it off. She was left in soaked panties and nothing else. She waited with trembling anticipation for his next move.

Without any warning, Tair leaned down and put his mouth over her mound through the panties. He licked against her clit and then gently sucked. She moaned and tried to lift to get more pressure. She wanted his mouth without anything in the way. He was making her crazy with need.

He moved one big hand and untied her panties on one side. Then, watching silently, he untied the other string. He used one finger to pull the panties down and away. They landed between her legs on the bed. She arched upward again, silently asking for what she wanted.

The heated look he gave her froze her in place. He said in a controlled voice, "You will not move or I will not touch you."

Kate frowned in response. She was wet and she was aching. He'd better touch her soon. She wanted to fight him, but at the same time she was too aroused to think of a plan at the moment. She could make him pay later.

When she remained silent, he seemed to take it as assent. Still looking into her eyes, he asked roughly, "Do you want my cock? Should I strip off these garments and plunge into you now? I want to feel your wet walls gripping me, Kate. I want to be inside you."

She shut her eyes at the image his words brought to mind. She opened them again. Gathering her strength, she said shakily, "No."

He stared hard at her and then asked shortly, "Do you want my mouth?"

Kate shuddered at his words. She wanted to feel him licking her. He knew exactly how to lick and to suck. Her sex clenched in anticipation. She nodded in response.

He took one finger and circled her clit in a teasing motion. In a cool voice, he said, "I am not sure that is really what you need."

She closed her eyes in frustration and then opened them again. She was beginning to get angry. "Would you just get on with it?"

Tair rocked back onto his knees and turned his head. Kate watched as the strange object he had gotten from the wall earlier floated through the air and came to rest in his hand. With a sense of unreality, she waited to see what would happen next.

Tair leaned forward and thrust two fingers into her tight sheath. Her head went back and she let out a long, low moan. He said, "You are so wet. Feel how my fingers slide in easily and fill you."

Kate could feel his long fingers thrusting in and out of her swollen sex. She was on fire and heading closer to the edge. She wanted more.

Instead of giving it to her, Tair removed his fingers. She bit back an instinctive protest, feeling cheated. Raising her head, she could see him watching her.

He stared into her eyes. Circling one finger around her opening, he murmured huskily, "Imagine how hard my cock would be inside you. How it would feel thrusting into you." He used both fingers and stabbed deep within her suddenly.

Kate's head fell back and she moaned loudly. He was tormenting her with sensual skill. She shook her head negatively from side to side, denying his seductive invitation. She was hanging on by a thread, but she refused to give in to intercourse. He pulled out his fingers and she nearly screamed at the frustration of it.

Suddenly, she felt a hard object probing deep within her. Opening her eyes, she raised her head and exclaimed, "What the hell?"

The object was cool and hard and growing inside her. It expanded until she was stretched and full. She bit her lip and took a few gasping breaths. It felt incredible. She looked at Tair and silently asked the question.

Tair smiled, although it looked strained. "It is a *mityb*, a Shimerian sex toy. It is perfectly safe. I will remove it later."

He sat up and began climbing off the bed. Kate watched in total disbelief. They weren't finished.

Tair turned back to her and said calmly, "Yes, Kate, for the moment we are finished."

Kate felt fury battle sharply with her arousal. He had gotten her into this state and then deliberately walked away. It made her want to hit something. She sat up abruptly and took several deep breaths. He was making a fool out of her.

Tair shook his head and said gently, "Kate, you must trust me. You will understand why I stopped later. I promise you. Right now, we have an agreement to explore my world. Remember?"

Kate knew she couldn't take the damn thing out. It was wedged inside her. It wasn't uncomfortable, but there was no way she could get it out on her own. And no way was she going to ask the intergalactic asshole either.

Feeling angry and frustrated, she vowed he would pay. He would feel ten times what she was feeling now. She'd make sure of it. She concentrated on regaining her control. Sexual games were not nearly as appealing at the moment as they'd seemed at the Oath ceremony. Climbing off the bed, she said coldly, "If we're going out, I need to put on another outfit."

Tair said, "I will be waiting outside." He turned and left the room. She heard him put on his boots in the living room. The front door opened and then slid shut.

Muttering, "You are going to be *so* sorry for this," she walked over to the wall and pressed the button for the closet. As it opened, she asked aloud, "What's the skimpiest thing in here?"

* * * * *

Tair stood outside and took deep gulps of fresh air. He was dying. His cock felt like it would burst out of his pants. It ached intensely, painfully. It had taken every ounce of control he possessed to walk away from her. He wiped the sweat from his brow and tried to relax.

Kate deserved her fantasy. He would not let anything get in the way, including his own desire. Reminding himself that she had only been on Shimeria a short time did not help.

He grimaced. When he finally fucked her, he was not going to stop for two days. With a self-mocking smile, he knew he would be lucky to last two seconds. He wanted her so much he was in complete agony. Kate would be pleased.

Chapter 8

Kate was not pleased. The intergalactic idiot had made a fool out of her. She was left frustrated and panting while he walked away coolly. There was no way he could be so unaffected. She had seen that slow "I-have-an-erection-so-hard-and-painful-I-can-barely-move" walk and the lines of strain on his face.

The dark blue halter top and skirt were skimpy enough to make him suffer. If not, he was inhuman. With a grimace at her word choice, she pondered her outfit. The strappy sandals only emphasized the length of her legs. She had even left off her panties.

The hologram had surprised her that morning, but she was beginning to see the benefits as opposed to a mirror. The three-dimensional image in front of her showed a woman who looked highly seductive and extremely dangerous. She took down her hair and watched it fall into soft, tempting waves. Perfect. She turned and left the room.

Her stomach gave a loud rumble just as she walked through the door and outside. Shooting Tair a scathing look, she said, "I suppose your next idea of fun is taking me to a banquet and starving me to death."

Seeing her step through the doorway in the skimpy outfit hit Tair like a physical punch. She literally took his breath away. Quickly, he worked to hide his reaction. She was determined to make him suffer. Tair smiled wryly. She was going to be difficult to appease. He would have to charm her in a hurry or at least distract her.

Reaching out, he grabbed her hand and began walking. Looking down at her he asked, "What do you think of our home from the outside?"

Kate stopped as she realized she was really standing on another planet. Outside. Looking around, she saw houses in rows like on earth. They were intersected by black walkways. Each house was made of some kind of pink material and had etchings on the front.

The etchings were beautiful. Most were strange landscapes, although she spotted one of an animal in flight further down the street. There was no grass, just a heavy blanketing foliage of thick, white leaves with small pink flowers. It was incredibly beautiful.

The temperature was comfortably warm. She had been to Hawaii once, and it felt lush and beautiful like this place. The colors here seemed even more vibrant, though. It was strange and alien but the beauty of it moved her in some indefinable way.

Tair saw Kate's eyes widen in wonder and felt something inside melt. She touched him so unexpectedly with her emotional responses. She tried so hard to be cold and unfeeling, but then her eyes would light up or go soft with hurt.

She was complex and surprising. Having been in her mind, he knew the beauty of her spirit and some of the causes of those defenses. He wanted to see her laughing with joy without any concern for restraint or appearances. He wanted to banish the hurt lurking inside her.

With a mental groan, he wondered if he was losing his mind. When she turned suddenly and gave him a blinding smile of pure joy, he could have sworn he heard his heart hit the ground at her feet with a thud.

Throwing up a quick block, he worked at keeping his composure. He was getting overly emotional, he chided inwardly. He was acting like a female or a mooning lovesick boy. It was ridiculous.

He was a Guardian and a warrior, and he did not spend time thinking about feelings. In an abrupt movement, he started walking again, tugging her along.

Kate was busy looking around her and trying to keep up with his long strides. She said with exasperation, "Excuse me, are we in a hurry or something all of a sudden?"

Tair nodded briskly, "Yes, we need to go. You are hungry. We will go to the eatery and get you something to eat. Now. While you are hungry."

Kate gave him a puzzled frown. He was very withdrawn and distant, even flustered. It was unlike him to repeat himself and he sounded...weird. Realizing she no longer felt him in her head, she said with some surprise, "You're blocking me."

Studying her surroundings moments before, she had been wrapped in a feeling of protection and warmth, his feelings soothing her. Then, Tair had some kind of moody moment, but she wasn't sure what had happened.

It had felt like a storm of emotion, with no one emotion that she could pick clearly. With a shrug, she said, "I don't know why you jumped back out of my head, but I appreciate it."

Tair said simply, "You are welcome." The two of them continued walking. Kate asked questions occasionally, but was met with short, absent-minded replies. Tair was plotting, she felt sure of it. He was acting strangely. With a mental shrug, she fell silent until they reached what was obviously a commercial area.

The buildings were much larger than the private houses. On the outside, there were carvings depicting the activities inside. As they walked toward one of them showing people eating, she asked, "What's the name of this place?"

Tair focused fully on Kate again. His thoughts had been running in circles. He needed to put them aside. With renewed determination he smiled. "*Yginfa's*. The food is excellent. It is an entertaining place. I do not think you will be disappointed."

Kate was ready for lunch. Breakfast had been a kind of hit-and-miss adventure, but the fruit hadn't lasted long. She was hungry and a little tired from their walk. She realized with some amazement she had nearly forgotten the *mityb* inside her. It was comfortable. It didn't really impede her in any way. It didn't slide around or press too hard either. Wondering how the Shimerians had figured that one out was something she filed away for another day.

Tair walked through the archway of the building. Kate stepped through behind him and paused as her eyes adjusted. The place was huge. There were around 75 tables, maybe even more.

The tables were occupied by Shimerian males mostly, although she could see many couples among the crowd. It was rather overwhelming as so many eyes turned to stare at her. She silently cursed the halter and short skirt, although the females were wearing similar outfits.

A waiter came forward. "*Ishaala* da'Kamon, welcome. If you will follow me, please?"

Tair nodded and followed the waiter to a table off to the left. There was a bench along the wall, with the table standing in front of it. Tair motioned for her to sit there and she slid into place. He slid in beside her. There were two chairs in front of the table on the opposite side as well.

The tables were covered with a thick cloth that looked heavier than cotton. They were light blue and went all the way to the floor. The entire inner walls of the building had carvings that looked like a tropical rainforest in full bloom, although a lot of the leaves were a very light blue color. It was gorgeous. Kate studied the walls in silent appreciation.

The waiter smiled and asked politely, "Your order, *Ishaala*?"

As the waiter and Tair began speaking in Shimerian, Kate considered the arrogance of him not consulting her about her preferences. Of course, he knew what she liked. The damnable man had been in her head.

Besides, it wasn't as if she could read the language if the waiter handed her a menu. Nor did there seem to be a menu. And what food would she pick? She had no idea. It gave her a weird feeling to hear the conversations going on around her in Shimerian. With a strange disorientation, she realized *she* was the real alien here.

The waiter nodded and strolled away to the other side of the room. She presumed he was headed toward the archway on that side. Watching him disappear through it, she looked around at the rest of the restaurant. There was another archway to the far left corner, too. She watched as several couples and small groups of threes walked through it.

Tair said suddenly, "It will not be long. In the meantime, I must apologize for my inattention during our walk."

Kate turned and looked at him. He looked genuinely sorry. With a shrug, she said calmly, "No problem. You're entitled to have a weird mood sometimes."

Tair smiled in relief. Cupping a hand over her cheek, he asked, "Am I so easily forgiven?"

Kate pulled away from the tender touch. With a shrug, she said coolly and with emphasis, "For your inattention during the walk, yes."

His withdrawal in the bedroom had really injured her, he realized with regret. He wondered if her fantasy would lift that hurt. He hoped fervently that it would. He reached out and wrapped both arms around her, giving her a hard hug. When she remained stiff, he pulled back and said quietly, sincerely, "I am very sorry that I hurt you."

Kate studied his expression. His sincerity eased some of her hurt. She still smarted at the thought of his withdrawal from their intimacy, but it was more injured pride now than anything else. Whatever his intentions, he had not meant to hurt her or make a fool of her. She nodded slowly, feeling uncomfortably vulnerable.

The waiter returned at that moment, bearing a large tray. He put two dark blue plates on the table along with matching cups. Setting bowls and platters in front of them, he looked at Tair. "Is everything to your satisfaction?"

Tair said, "Thank you, Rijhem. It looks wonderful." The waiter beamed in response. With a nod to her and then to Tair, he left them and walked back across the room.

Kate picked up her cup and peered at the liquid inside. It was the same color of blue as the cup. Blinking slowly, she said, "I was afraid of that."

Tair smiled. "*Permu* is quite good, much like one of your fruit punches. I think you will enjoy it."

Kate lifted the cup to her lips and took a cautious sip. It was slightly sweet and refreshing. She was startled that it fizzed a little in her mouth. Setting it back down, she looked at the unrecognizable things in dishes on the table.

Each dish held a substance formed into small shapes. Some were oval, while others were square. They were oddly colored, too. Some appeared to be meat from the darker color, but there was no way to know. Feeling indecisive, she wondered where to start.

Tair smiled and picked up a square. Handing it to her, he said, "This is *hefdarsa*. I believe you will like it."

For the next hour she and Tair sampled the various foods. He told her the Shimerian names and answered her questions about the dishes. It was pleasant and relaxing for both of them. The armed atmosphere between the two of them, usually so predominant, disappeared gradually as they talked and laughed.

For Kate, it was a revelation. She had known he could be charming, but she was surprised at how good she felt talking with him. The conversation slipped from food to other interests. In a number of ways, they were amazingly alike.

They both hated the new Earth music, preferring the old classics instead. Both loved museums and were passionate about their work. She knew he was a Guardian, similar to a cop on Earth, but she was impressed with his dedication to the job.

He thought of it as a duty and felt it was important that he use his abilities to make a difference in his world. She felt the same way about her job. He mentioned the need for Earth lawyers at the judicial building created by the mixing of the two cultures. She narrowed her eyes at him, and he quickly changed the subject.

Finally, Kate leaned back against the booth and sighed in contentment. She was feeling so much better. Looking around, she saw that the lunch crowd had thinned. This had been a surprisingly nice meal.

Then, Tair put a casual arm around her shoulders and whispered quietly in her ear, "Kate, I think you should experience that fantasy now."

Kate turned her head, nearly bumping into him. He drew back a little just in time. She asked, "What fantasy? What do you mean?"

Tair said calmly, "Look straight ahead."

Kate was totally confused. All she saw were the other diners in the restaurant. Nothing had changed. It was less crowded, but there were still a lot of people. There was nothing to see. She heard Tair whisper in her ear, "We are in a crowded room full of strangers. When you come, remember not to scream."

Kate's eyes widened in complete shock. Her throat went dry. Memories of heated fantasies involving the thrill of near discovery flashed through her head. She had one in particular, involving a public place. Surely, he wouldn't try to do anything here. It was insane.

Tair tightened his arm around her shoulders in a restraining grip. "I am going to talk to you and you are going to nod at me occasionally. Unless you do something to call attention, no one will know."

The last word was no sooner out of his mouth than the *mityb* inside her started to vibrate. "Oh my God," she exclaimed, keeping her voice down desperately. "You have got to be kidding."

The *mityb* vibrated harder against the inner walls of her sex. There was no sound, no buzz. Tiar was using his power to do it. He was controlling it inside her with delicate skill. Feeling shaken to the core, she closed her eyes and said, "I can't handle this here."

Tair gave a quiet chuckle. "Yes, Kate, you can and you will."

The vibration picked up more speed. Kate looked around wildly. No one was paying any attention to them in the least. She felt a growing arousal and fought for control. This was crazy. She might have thought about something like this before, but she had never thought to actually do it. Okay, she had thought about it a lot, but this could not be happening.

Biting her lip, she felt arousal spread through her body like a fever. She was getting hot. Her nipples tightened and she felt the moisture gathering between her legs. Pressing her legs together, she tried to dim the sensation and regain control.

Tair said firmly, "Spread your legs."

She shot him a helpless look and shook her head. She felt a rising hysteria at the thought of getting caught.

Tair ordered, "Compliance, Kate. Spread them. No one can see. No one will know. Spread them now for me or I will push you until you scream for release."

Kate trembled. The ache to climax was growing larger. The *mityb* was vibrating and expanding inside her, filling her in a way that she could not have imagined in any fantasy. Slowly, she spread her legs. The vibration became more intense.

Tair said quietly, "Now, *sheka*, focus on the far wall above everyone here. Remember to nod occasionally so the others do not grow suspicious or assume I am a poor companion." She could hear the smile in his voice as he said that last part.

She looked at the etching on the far wall and focused on a large red flower. She felt a flush rising on her neck and face as she struggled to maintain control. The damn thing was hitting her G-spot perfectly. She fought the impulse to drop her head back and just let go.

Tair made a little hum of approval. "Good. Now reach down and play with your clit."

Kate thought she was beyond shock, but evidently she wasn't. She shook her head no in a jerky movement.

Tair took her right hand and laid it in her lap, bringing the tablecloth forward to cover the movement. She heard his voice close to ear as he said softly, "Touch yourself. Do it. It will feel very good."

Kate was lost in a haze of desire. She was getting desperate to climax and was terrified it would show if she did. The fear of being discovered fought with the heat of her arousal. She felt afraid to let go and yearned for it at the same time.

With a tentative movement, she let her hand wander down until it rested on the fabric of her skirt over her mound. With sudden recklessness, she probed. The cloth became drenched in a matter of minutes. The feel of her finger and the texture of the cloth as she played with her clit nearly made her eyes roll back in her head.

She was on fire and out of control. The vibration of the *mityb* increased with the speed of her fingers. The pleasure was so intense, she could barely think. She trembled and worried about crying out.

Tair whispered, "Remember not to scream, Kate. They will know what is happening if you do."

Kate whimpered, but it was no use. Her sex clenched and she felt the beginning pulses of release. She bit her lip hard. The *mityb* continued to vibrate as ripples of pleasure spread through her. Helplessly, she opened her mouth to scream.

Tair grabbed her chin roughly and planted his mouth over hers. Her scream was lost in an intense, tongue-thrusting kiss. She shuddered and he wrapped both arms around her. As the last ripple of pleasure passed, she realized in relief that it would look like a passionate embrace to any diners observing them. They had no way of knowing what had happened. The intensity of her orgasm left her feeling shattered and weak. The *mityb* slowed to a stop.

Tair shifted uncomfortably on the bench as he held Kate close. The aching pain of his hard cock made him want to howl with frustration. He pushed her head into his shoulder and said, "Breath. I will hold you until you recover." He turned and placed a kiss near the top of her head into her hair.

Eventually, she was able to pull back from him. She felt nearly boneless, but her brain was beginning to function. Unfortunately, she couldn't think of a single thing to say. At all. The orgasm had been so unbelievable.

Tair smiled, looking down at her. She looked flushed and sleepily satisfied but otherwise okay. His tone was part tease, part concern, as he asked, "Was it worth the wait?"

Her smile when it emerged could have lit an entire planet. Her eyes were glowing. As if remembering herself, she made an attempt at giving him a look of reproof by narrowing her eyes and turning her lips down in a frown.

However, she couldn't hold the expression, and gave him a big grin instead. Joy bloomed in his chest at that smile. Tair threw back his head and laughed. With a huge grin, he said, "I believe that means yes."

Suddenly, a large body stood in front of their table. There was a buzz as conversation grew louder in the immediate vicinity. Curious, both Kate and Tair turned and looked up. Jadik stood in front of them, wearing a smile of his own.

Chapter 9

Tair exclaimed, "Jadik, hello! Please join us."

Kate heard the words and was utterly appalled. She pulled away from Tair abruptly and straightened until her back was ramrod straight. Crossing her legs, she wondered frantically if what she'd been doing would be apparent under those sharp eyes.

She knew her face was still flushed. As Jadik's smile grew wider, she felt the flush deepen. She lifted her chin and glared at him in response.

Jadik said with friendly good humor, "Hello, Tair. Hello, Kate. If you are sure I am not intruding, I would like to join you." His dark eyes sparkled with mirth.

Tair said, "Of course you are not intruding. Kate and I have just finished..."

Kate made a small choking sound, caught between horror and protest. He ended with "...midmeal."

Jadik nodded and slid his big body into the chair across the table from them, studying her flushed face with obvious interest. Nodding over his shoulder to the waiter who was headed his way, Jadik turned and asked, "Kate, how was the meal? I have found the food here to be ... quite satisfying." His tone was conversational, but those wicked eyes danced.

Kate was spared a reply when the waiter arrived. While Jadik was occupied with the waiter for a moment, Kate leaned toward Tair and whispered in furious undertones, "Do you think he knows what we were doing? He's just trying to goad me, right? It doesn't show. Tell me it doesn't show."

Tair gave a choked laugh. In an equally low voice, he said, "Kate, now might be the time to mention the exceptional hearing of Shimerians. He could not have known for sure, but now I believe you have told him."

Kate gave a strangled moan and shut her eyes. When she opened them, the waiter was gone, and Jadik was grinning at her in open amusement. "I was right then. Your meal was exceptional." He threw back his head and laughed.

Tair joined in because he couldn't help it. Kate looked so flustered. She was trying so hard to look coolly sophisticated, but instead she only looked more adorably uncomfortable. She looked nothing like the coldly remote Kate she was usually so careful to present to the world.

He leaned down and placed a firm kiss on her mouth. Lifting his head, he said, "Kate, relax. Everything is fine. You look beautiful. We are having a good time. Jadik is teasing you. It is one of his favorite pastimes."

Seeing the humor in the situation suddenly, Kate relaxed. In the aftermath of her orgasm it was just too much work to be cool and composed. So what if Jadik knew something had happened? They were all adults. Besides, he couldn't know exactly what had occurred.

Tossing her hair back over her shoulder, she grinned and said, "It was fabulous. The entertainment alone is worth the price of the meal."

Both men's eyes widened in surprise and then they all laughed. The waiter brought more drinks and the light tone of the conversation was set. Tair and Jadik tossed out possible suggestions for what Kate might like to see next on Shimeria.

They argued agreeably about which sights were too commercial or overpriced. Kate asked numerous questions and they answered her diligently. It was a friendly, amusing exchange.

As the minutes passed, Kate noticed she was feeling even more incredibly relaxed. Peering into the empty bottom of her cup, she said enthusiastically, "I think I need a refill. Man, am I thirsty. Is that my fourth? Oh, wait, I have a joke I want to share."

A worried frown darkened Tair's brow. He looked at her closely. Jadik leaned forward and studied her, too. They were staring at her in fascination like she was an animal at the zoo. She gave an indignant sniff in response. She asked, "What's the difference between a Shimerian and a lawyer?"

When neither man answered, she smiled broadly and said proudly, "None. They'll both fuck you in a heartbeat."

She felt great. For some reason, the joke struck her as hilarious and she laughed until her shoulders shook and tears came to her eyes. That was a good one. When neither man laughed, she asked, "Don't you get it?"

Tair felt a creeping resignation come over him. He should have known. He shook his head in sheer disbelief.

Jadik leaned toward him and said pointedly, "She must be allergic to the *permu*. I saw someone react this way once and it was the same."

Tair shook his head in resignation. "Of course. She fainted when she came through the portal. I should have guessed she would be one of the rare ones to react to *permu*, too."

Kate piped up indignantly, "I collapsed with fatigue."

Tair rolled his eyes. "Fine. You were one of the rare ones to collapse with fatigue."

Kate studied the two men. They were acting way too serious. Jadik looked confused. Tair looked resigned. Kate felt wonderful. Giving them a big grin, she asked, "What's the matter, Jadik? Not smugly all-knowing for once?"

Tair winced. "Kate, you are allergic to *permu*. One cup or two does not have any effect, but you have had more since Jadik joined us. The side effects are extreme elation and relaxation. It will pass quickly as your body fully metabolizes it, but in the meantime, you must endure."

Under his breath, he muttered, "We must endure."

Kate lifted her chin. "Are you accusing me of being drunk? Is this stuff" she slammed the cup on the table with a loud *thump*, "alcoholic? Don't be ridiculous. I don't ever get drunk."

Jadik couldn't decide whether to laugh or to try to reason with Kate. Tair was looking helpless. Trying for a straight face, he said, "No, you are not drunk. Well, you are relaxed and feeling drunk, but your motor skills are fine. You are..."

He searched for the words. "...merely a more relaxed, looser version of yourself."

Seeing her instant frown, he added, "I find it quite charming."

Tair chimed in quickly, "As do I. "

Kate studied the two of them suspiciously. They looked kind of sweet. Like two small boys trying to please her. With a grin, she asked, "So you're saying I'm myself, only squared?"

Jadik muttered, "More like Kate Cubed" under his breath, but he nodded in response. He and Tair both waited anxiously for her reply.

Kate shrugged and said brightly, "Excellent. And I was right. I needed the algebra after all."

Tair and Jadik had no idea what she was talking about and looked totally confused. Kate didn't care, she was off and running. "You know," she leaned back and threw one arm along the back of the bench, "Planet Kink is rather beautiful so far, Jadik. It has some nasty surprises, but overall I find it strangely compelling."

Both men nodded their heads in cautious agreement. She stared thoughtfully at Jadik a moment and then added, "Rather like you."

Jadik's eyes widened. He didn't know whether to be insulted or not. In careful tones, he said, "Errr, thank you, Kate. I think."

She nodded brightly and gave a nod toward Tair. She said with carefree good humor, "Don't worry. He doesn't mind me saying it. He's not jealous at all. He's been nagging me about this linking thing." She rolled her eyes.

Tair held onto his patience. Torn between laughing and gritting his teeth. Linking was one subject he thought it best to avoid at the moment. So, of course, Kate continued.

Kate was thinking about the whole linking thing. Really, it didn't seem like such a big deal. She and Tair would do the wild thing and Jadik would jump in when necessary with a quick body hug. She tried to picture the three of them and felt her whole body go hot in response.

Tair looked at Jadik and saw his friend shift in discomfort. Kate was broadcasting amazing sexual images of the three of them. Jadik had to be catching some of them. They were certainly powerful and graphic enough.

Shaking his head, he stood up abruptly. He caught Jadik's eye and said, "I think Kate needs...dessert."

Jadik looked startled briefly and then followed his lead. "Of course." As understanding hit him, he said more enthusiastically, "I believe you are right."

Kate frowned. She might be able to squeeze in a little dessert, but she was somewhat full. She watched as Jadik stood, too. Tair leaned down and took her arm gently. She rose slowly and carefully, but then realized there was no need. Her balance was perfectly fine.

She asked, "We have to stand for dessert here? Is this another weird custom? Let me guess, we need to strip before we can eat it, too."

She sighed. Whatever. This was such a kinky planet. Her hand went to her blouse. "When in Rome..."

Tair grabbed her hand quickly and began walking with her toward the archway at the back. It was the one other people had disappeared into earlier. Kate asked, "You have a separate dessert room? Now that is just strange."

Tair gave an exasperated laugh and said as they continued walking, "Kate, as soon as we get there, I will explain. Please follow me."

In a lightening change of mood, she said, "Yeah, and you've done such a bang-up job of explaining everything so far." Elation gave way to frustration. She felt pissed.

She was tired of being confused. She was tired of being on another planet dependent upon Tair to guide her and explain. She was no one's dependent anything. With mounting anger, she entered the next room.

There were buttons spaced out in even intervals along one continuous wall. Some buttons were lit up purple and others were green. Frowning, she said, "What is it with you people and the button fetish? Are doors just too primitive a concept to master? You have wallways instead of doorways. This planet makes no sense."

Tair pressed the purple button closest to them. The wall folded in upon itself to reveal a medium – sized room. There were shelves running the length of the room on three walls. There were a wide variety of foods sitting on the shelves. Some of it was in dishes, while others were piled up like fruit. She asked, "We eat in some kind of dessert pantry without tables or chairs?"

Jadik entered the room behind her and pressed the button on the wall behind him to close the door.

She watched as Tair and Jadik moved to opposite sides of the room. Jadik picked up a red fruit of some kind.

Tair picked up a fruit that was a bright green color. By the way he held it, she could tell it was squishy and ripe. Walking over to her, he held it to her mouth and said calmly, "Bite."

Willing and curious, Kate took a bite. The taste was delicious. It had the mushy texture of overripe banana, but it tasted similar to a tangerine. She smiled. "I like it."

Tair said, "Good." He smiled back and then smashed it on her chest.

Kate froze. He hadn't hurt her, but the shock of it held her in place. Tair had just smashed green fruit on her. Giving him a lethal glare, she said, "You absolutely did not do that."

His grin widened in response. Suddenly, a piece of red fruit landed with a splat against the side of his head. Watching it slide down his neck with a slimy trail, she smiled smugly and turned to Jadik.

She called out, "Thank you, Jadik" just as a second red piece hit her squarely in the chest. She clenched her hands and added, "You jerk."

Tair spun around and ran over to a shelf. Grabbing another piece of fruit, he called out, "Kate, why are you waiting?"

They were crazy. The two of them were lobbing fruit back and forth at each other like snowballs. It was insane. As another piece hit her on one leg, she said calmly, "You are going to be so sorry for that."

Walking over to the corner, she grabbed a couple of fruits at random. Hefting a larger orange one like a baseball, she threw it at Tair with all her strength. It hit him in the back of the head. He spun around in surprise.

She said smugly, "I was a starting pitcher for ten years. Prepare to die, nitwit."

Hefting the other orange fruit at Jadik, she hit him right in the forehead. Jadik laughed and hit her on the other leg with a purple one, close to her crotch. The battle was on. The three of them threw food until their arms ached and their sides hurt from laughing. It was the biggest mess Kate had ever seen in her life. It was also one of the greatest moments of sheer goofy fun she could remember.

Finally, Kate sank down onto the floor and propped her back against the wall. As stuff oozed down her face and neck, she brought her hand up and scooped it off. She started to toss it away, and then brought it to her mouth. Eyes widening in surprise, she realized it was actually quite good.

Tair sank down next to her, laughing. Scooping a small portion off his sleeve, he brought it to his mouth and chewed. He turned to her and said with a grin, "I forgot about your being a pitcher. I believe I have received my share of dessert."

Kate laughed. He was covered head to toe just as much as she was, if not more. Jadik sank down in front of them and licked a stray piece of fruit off of his hand.

With a lusty grin, he said in a mock Kate-voice, "Prepare to die, nitwit."

He laughed uproariously and then said, "Kate, you have a great style. I have not laughed so hard in a long time."

She tossed her head, although the effect was lost somewhat as sticky strands stuck to her neck. In a mock-Jadik sultry voice, she said, "It is my pleasure, " and winked.

Both men burst out laughing. Kate grinned. She wasn't feeling drunk anymore, but she felt just plain good. Somehow, the ultimate food fight had helped her regain her balance. She felt relaxed and comfortable in a way that was totally unexpected.

The only other times she ever felt like this was when she was with Sharon or Gage. Men bonded in the weirdest ways, she reminded herself. They were weird creatures and Shimerian males were stranger than most. But, there was still something nice in the camaraderie she felt. Bonding by food fight. It was a new concept, but apparently affective.

The three of them sat in comfortable silence for a minute, eating the fruit they gathered from themselves. Finally, Jadik stood and said, "I am afraid I must go. Tair, I have been most entertained. It has been a pleasure." He threw a mock fierce look at Kate.

Kate and Tair stood. Kate grinned as Jadik walked over to her and stared down. She felt her smile begin to fade as she saw him hesitate. He turned to Tair for a second and then looked back down at her. Placing both hands around her face, he raised it and brought his mouth down.

Kate froze in shock. Jadik was kissing her. His firm lips moved gently as he patiently sought a response. She felt her body grow warm and was appalled. She tried to pull back, but his hands held her firmly in place. He ran his tongue teasingly along the seam of her mouth. She kept her mouth closed firmly and grasped for control.

In a sudden move, he took one hand away from her face. Wrapping his arm around her back, he pulled her forward into his body. She opened her mouth to protest and he thrust his tongue boldly inside. Feeling like she was losing a battle, she fought to control the instinctive impulse to respond.

Finally, she answered his tongue with her own. They shared a hot, fruit-flavored kiss, and then Jadik pulled back. Wiping her hair back off her forehead with a gentle hand, he gazed at her with dark eyes and said huskily, "Welcome to Shimeria, Kate. I am honored to be your link."

Kate was stunned. Wrenching away guiltily, she took a step back and looked at Tair in confusion. He was looking at the two of them, but his expression was calm. He smiled and said casually, "Kate, I believe it is time for us to depart as well."

Kate said stiffly, "I have not agreed to link."

She was so confused. Her emotions were in a tangle. Tair was blocking her again, so she had no idea how he felt. She couldn't even begin to sort out her own emotions.

Jadik smiled. "I will see you both soon."

Walking over to Tair, he clasped his hand on his shoulder. Tair mirrored the action. She heard the two speak in Shimerian in rapid, low tones. This being on another planet and not able to speak the language was damned inconvenient. She resolved to spend more time at the tutorial soon.

She watched as Jadik nodded to Tair and then turned and walked to the wall. Pressing the button, he walked out.

Kate didn't want to discuss what had happened just yet. She was feeling off-balance and unsure. She turned to Tair and said crisply, "Tell me we don't have to clean up this mess."

She was recovering fast. His Kate was a fighter. In mournful tones, Tair said, "I am afraid that we do."

Kate felt her heart stop. Looking around at the disastrous state of the room, she said flatly, "That is information I could have used an hour ago."

Tair laughed and walked over to gather her in a hug. Smiling widely, he said, "I am joking, *sheka*. Others will come to clean the mess. We need only clean ourselves."

Kate looked at the two of them. She was covered in fruit and so was he. She arched an eyebrow. "And just how do we do that?"

Tair said, "Please follow me."

Following him out of the room, she muttered, "So you said before. I believe those were the words that made me a walking fruit salad." The absurdity of the situation struck her forcibly. They both looked ridiculous. She smiled to herself as she walked.

Tair had been right. The entertainment at *Yginfa's* was great. The meal was good. Her bizarre drunken allergic reaction had passed without incident. Certainly, dessert had been unique.

She was coping rather well with life on Planet Kink. Jadik's kiss flashed into consciousness, but she pushed the thought away and filed it under, "To be dealt with later." Much later.

She felt the movement of the *mityb* still inside her as she walked. The memory of her orgasm passed through her mind and left arousal in its wake. It had been hotter than any of her fantasies, and incredibly intense. With a shimmer of anticipation, she wondered what Tair had in mind as his next sexual surprise.

A little voice in her head said that he had been wooing her carefully up until now. It was a clever strategy to tempt her into further intimacy and lull her into feeling in control. The voice cautioned that when he next pushed her, he would catch her by surprise and be even more difficult to resist.

With a mental grimace, she told the voice in her head to shut up. She was Kate Carson, and she could handle anything. The voice asked, "Even Tair?" but Kate refused to answer.

Tair's said loudly, "Kate, I have deducted our meal. We can reach the shower through here." He was standing next to an opening in the wall. They were still in the back part of the restaurant separate from the diners.

Tair gave her a questioning look as he motioned for her to enter the next room. He must have been trying to get her attention for some time while she was wrapped in her thoughts.

Kate looked at him and swallowed hard. Suddenly, he looked very big, very male, and very impatient. She looked down at herself, and realized her top and skirt were indecently plastered to her body. Her nipples were tight and obvious against the wet cloth.

Looking back at Tair, she lifted her chin. She began walking and said irritably, "I'm coming, I'm coming."

Tair gave her a slow, sexy smile in response. His eyes roamed her body with lazy appreciation. As she passed by him, he said with simple promise, "You will."

Chapter 10

Kate walked past Tair, suppressing a shudder at his words. Glancing around her, she saw a long hallway that appeared to run the length of the building. There were more buttons, of course.

Tair came up beside her and pushed a purple button. Purple must mean unoccupied, she surmised. The wall slid open to reveal a small room that was like one open shower stall. There were steps along the length of the walls like benches. There were hooks along the wall to the left.

She spotted a lever on the left too, off to one side, but she didn't see any showerheads. Looking up, she saw tiny nozzles all over the ceiling. She glanced at Tair and raised an eyebrow in question.

Tair said casually, "We can hang our garments on the hooks. They will be cleaned as we are cleaned. As you know from experience, the *vasa* dries within minutes."

Reaching for the hem of his shirt, he drew it up over his head and walked to one of the hooks. Kate watched the muscles ripple in his back and felt her mouth water. The man was being incredibly sexy without even realizing it. The sculptured contours of his muscular back and broad shoulders made her blood heat.

She stood there in silent appreciation as he hung up the shirt and then leaned down and removed his boots with quick economical motions. His hands moved to the front of his pants.

He was still facing away from her. She held her breath in anticipation of the view. As he peeled the pants downward over his legs, she watched his firm butt flex at the motion.

Evidently, he had left off underwear, too. She felt heat flow through her like a river. She was hot and she was aching, and she wanted him to turn around right now.

Tair turned and spotted Kate still standing, fully dressed. She was flushed and watching him with a look that was unmistakable. Her nipples were tight and protruding from the wet halter top. The outline of her sex was faintly visible under the skirt. She was looking at him like she wanted to devour him in one hungry bite.

His cock hardened painfully and throbbed in response. He tried to hold onto his control, but he had little remaining after being left hungry for Kate twice already today. Kate's eyes went to his cock and she licked her lips unconsciously. He could have sworn he heard the snap as his control broke. Walking to her in long strides, he planted his mouth over hers and gave her a hard, deep, wet kiss.

Kate felt her heart jump when Tair strode toward looking her like a man who had been pushed beyond all reason. He planted his mouth on hers and thrust his tongue inside in a deep hungry motion. She was lost in an instant, and eager for more.

Opening her mouth, she returned the kiss frantically, dueling with his tongue. Shifting closer to him, she felt his arms come around her in a rough embrace. This was no teasing seduction. It was pure aching need.

Kate pulled back and drew her blouse over her head. Pulling away from him, she took deep breaths in an attempt to slow down. He watched her with the gaze of a waiting predator.

She walked to the closest hook and hung the blouse on it. In a quick jerky motion she pulled the sandals from her feet and then stood up to remove the skirt. Pulling it over her hips quickly, she placed it with her blouse. Then, she turned and faced him.

Tair wasn't even conscious of walking to her. He knew he had to touch her, and then suddenly she was in his arms. Pulling her to him, he dipped his head and began to kiss her again. The touch of skin-against-skin made them both catch their breaths. Tair merged with her in one hard push.

Feeling his desire feed her own, Kate shuddered at the intensity of the feeling. The passion built between the two of them. She felt as if her entire body was heated from the inside out.

Kate moaned as Tair moved from her mouth and began licking and sucking on her neck. He was licking the juice from her body like a starving man. She shuddered at the wet velvet glide of his tongue over her skin. As he moved down to her breasts and sucked one hard nipple into his mouth, her legs went weak. His pleasure and need flowed into her in a continuous wave.

She pushed back from him and brought her mouth to his chest. The hard muscles jumped beneath her mouth and tongue as she licked and sucked. The tangy sweet flavors of the fruit were delicious combined with the taste of him. Tair went rigid as her roving mouth moved over him, except for his big hands stroking her back and shoulders.

Kate worked her way downward until she reached his navel. Placing biting kisses around it, she probed the tiny indention with her tongue. Tair moaned in response and his hands flexed on her back. His pleasure and intense desire swamped her.

Kate continued licking and kissing her way down and then abruptly went to her knees. She looked up. He was looking at her with heavy-lidded eyes dark with arousal. His face was tight and there was a flush along his cheekbones. He looked like he was holding his breath. She could literally feel his anticipation and need.

Kate leaned forward and took his hard length into her mouth. She heard him groan and looked upward to see his head fall back. His hands went to the back of her head and tangled in her hair. He was completely lost.

Feeling his incredible pleasure radiate to her, she moaned in response. She moved her mouth up and down his length in a slow sucking motion. He exclaimed huskily, "Kate!" as if asking for mercy.

His cock was huge and hard against the soft inside of her mouth and tongue. As she moved along its length, she could feel it throb in response. She brought her hands up and grabbed the cheeks of his butt, pulling him closer.

As she flexed her hands, she knew her nails were biting into him, but the tiny pain only enhanced his pleasure. His legs trembled. They both moaned. She continued tormenting him for several long moments, increasing the pressure of her mouth.

He warned gruffly, "Kate, I'm going to come" and made a motion as if to draw away. Instead, she pulled him closer and sucked him harder. She could feel his tension and the all-consuming need for release. He was breathing hard as if he had run a marathon and was in the last stretch.

Then, with a choking noise, she felt him go rigid. His spine arched and she felt the warmth of his seed in her mouth. Pleasure, powerfully intense and overwhelming hit her like a punch. As she swallowed, the intensity of his release triggered her own. Her sex clenched and pulsed as the blinding pleasure moved through her. She moaned and sank down to the floor. Tair sank down beside her and wrapped her in his arms. They held onto each other as they recovered.

Finally, Kate lifted her head. With a thoroughly relaxed smile, she teased, "And I didn't even have to be a mind-reader to guess your fantasy. We females are powerful and mysterious creatures."

With a huge grin, Tair said, "I believe this is one time that we are in absolute agreement. You may guess my fantasies whenever the mood occurs. I have no objections. You may seduce me at any time."

He said the last statement with such enthusiasm that Kate threw back her head and laughed. Her sticky hair reminded her that they still needed a shower. With a groan of regret, she said, "As much as I enjoyed dessert, we still need that shower."

Tair stood up reluctantly and held his hand out to her. She noticed another flash of amusement light his eyes. Taking his hand and getting up, she asked, "What's so funny?"

He grinned and his eyes sparkled. "You look good on your knees."

Kate shot him a narrow look and said tartly, "Well, I've had you on yours often enough, too."

He wrapped her in a hug. The nozzles overhead turned on in a sudden rush and Kate felt *vara* cascade over the two of them like a hard, warm rain. Tair had turned the lever telepathically.

Lifting her face, she laughed and enjoyed the feel of it on her skin. It was like being caught in a rain storm on a warm summer day. Taking a step back from Tair, she twirled and lifted her arms up with sheer pleasure.

Tair watched her and felt his breath catch in his throat. She looked so incredibly lovely and free. Her open happiness and childlike joy made his chest tight.

With chilling fear, he realized he could lose her. She could walk right out of his life after only two weeks. Shoving the thought from his mind, he pasted a smile on his face to cover his sudden panic. He was not letting her go.

With cold calculation, he began plotting. The only way to win with Kate was to lull her into feeling he was no threat, and then strike. She would think he was giving in to her wishes. It would be all the more effective when he pushed her in earnest.

She would be angry and feel betrayed when he upped the stakes, but it was a penalty that he would pay. For him, the game had turned deadly serious. He was not letting her go. Ever. He was going to win at any cost.

Chapter 11

A few days later, Kate leaned against the balcony railing and marveled at the beauty of the night around her. It was her fifth night in Shimeria, but the planet held her spell-bound still at times. Overhead, two huge moons glowed brilliant silver, lighting the darkness of the night.

She looked down at the dark shadow of the *Kuldelma* Lake below her and felt the cool breeze off the *vara*. She could hear the distant sounds of unfamiliar animals breaking the silence around her.

She and Tair might have been the only ones in the universe at the moment. It felt like that, at least. Lifting her hand, she studied the luminescent glow of her skin and wondered again what caused human skin to glow like a pearl at night under those big moons.

A masculine voice penetrated her thoughts, a few seconds before she felt strong arms wrap around her from behind. She felt Tair place a gentle kiss into her hair near the side of her forehead and smiled.

He said quietly, "I am glad you like it, *sheka*. I thought it would appeal to you. I have always enjoyed this place. It is special."

Kate leaned back into the warmth of his big body and half-turned to look up at him. His face was relaxed and his eyes were gentle. She said,

"Thank you, Tair. It's beautiful. Truly lovely. This was a very nice gift."

He smiled. The arms around her tightened briefly and then his eyes took on a devilish light. "I have brought you here with more than one motive. I must be honest."

She flashed him a look under her lashes. She felt mellow and strangely content. It had been one of the most perfect, romantic evenings she could ever remember in her life.

They had eaten a lovely dinner at a quiet eatery with dim lighting and soft music. He'd even given her a flower. A *kryji*. When he handed it to her in the restaurant, it was a small yellow bud. The waiter had brought a small container for her to use.

Tair had been charming and funny. It was only about fifteen minutes into the meal that she realized the flower was changing. She had watched with amazement as the bud bloomed. It had unfurled and turned from yellow to pink and then finally to brilliant beautiful red.

Remembering the simple beauty of it made her smile. Tair had looked at her when she thanked him for it again, and said simply, "It reminded me of you." Her heart softened yet again at the remembrance. Coming out of her reverie, she shook herself.

So, she wasn't entirely immune to mushy stuff, she admitted. If Tair wanted to play, she was ready. She grinned. "I have this fantasy…"

He laughed. "Yes, I know. I am depending upon it."

She shook her head in mock reproof and started to turn around to face him. She was surprised when his arms tightened just enough to keep her in place. She turned her head sideways and looked up at him.

Leaning her full weight against him, she felt his cock harden against the small of her back and her bottom. She saw his expression change from mischief to desire. Her mind filled with an image of him filling her from behind, and she drew a steadying breath.

They had skirted the sexual line for several days now – always stopping just short of intercourse. She had been left satisfied and yet still longing for the taste of the forbidden. It was a dangerous game they were playing, because the life consequences were very high for both. She knew neither one of them planned to lose, and yet one of them was bound to end up defeated. It wasn't going to be her, either.

He had tried to lure her, but didn't pursue aggressively. It was surprising. She felt half-relieved and half-disappointed at the same time. It was confusing. If he truly pressed her, would she be able to say no?

She shook off the disturbing thought. Her voice emerged in a husky whisper. "What exactly do you have in mind?"

He leaned down and whispered into her ear. "Lean forward and put your hands on the top of the rail and I will answer your question."

His arms loosened. She swallowed and ran her tongue over her suddenly dry lips. She felt wet already and they had barely begun. How far would it go? How hard would he push? Her mind flashed danger signs but her body was aching and anxious to find out. With a mental shrug, she planted her hands on the rail and waited in expectant silence.

Her tension climbed higher when he did not make any immediate move. She felt the cool breeze caress her body through the thin halter and short skirt and shivered slightly as it traveled over the heat of her skin. She felt him move forward and place his hands over hers. She felt surrounded by him. It was intoxicating.

She felt his mouth against the side of her neck and she moved her head in response to accommodate him. He began placing nibbling kisses along the skin right below her chin. It felt so good.

He said between small bites and licks, "Do not move them. Keep them there."

She drew in a deep breath. Her nipples were aching for his hands and his mouth already. With a little moan, she said, "Okay."

As if to reward her, he removed his hands and placed them on her stomach. The heat of his palms warmed her through the thin material of the skirt and blouse. As he continued stroking lazily, traveling upward, she waited anxiously for the touch of his hands on her breasts. He continued the leisurely movements until she was ready to scream at him to touch her nipples.

His voice was husky as he said, "Easy, Kate. Relax for me now and simply enjoy. You must do nothing except feel the pleasure of your body beneath my touch. You have no control and no responsibility."

She closed her eyes at the sound of those words. He knew what he was doing. This was seduction on an entirely different level. She remembered lonely nights in the dark touching her aching sex, imagining a lover who would take her slowly.

A lover who would know just how to touch and when. An encounter where she could just relax completely and be pleasured. No worrying about the other person. No responsibility or control. Just pleasure. She felt her knees go weak as she realized that Tair was going to give her that fantasy.

She swallowed hard and tried to speak, but could think of nothing to say. Her mind was filled with the heat of his hands on her body. She felt them cup her breasts and moaned helplessly. He kneaded them softly for a moment, making her bite her lip at the delicious torment. She wanted those fingers on her aching nipples. She choked out, "Oh...I can't...Just touch me..."

Tair said in a firmer voice, "Kate, let go. I mean what I say."

He thumbed her nipples through the halter with slow circles and she moved into his hands. Her back arched and she gripped the rail harder. He was killing her slowly. She wanted more. She needed more.

He said gruffly, "Step back a little and spread your legs. Do not move your hands."

She could feel the night around her, but her world was narrowing down to his voice and his hands. Without a sound, she did as he asked, and waited. She was bent forward now, the balcony hard and cold beneath the grip of her hands. In sharp contrast, she felt warm from her head to her toes. She demanded, "More."

He made a low noise in his throat at her demand, as if in pain, but his voice was teasing and seductive, "Here, Kate?"

His fingers tugged gently on her nipples. She opened her eyes and her head came up. She muttered, "Yes..."

He continued playing with her nipples, making her ache. She was dripping wet. Her sex ached with the need to have his cock inside her. Her inner voice screamed caution.

She knew with sudden certainty that she was in trouble. She was losing control and it was dangerous. She started to move upward and remove her hands, but the sharp bark of his voice kept her immobile. "Compliance, Kate. Remember?"

She nodded slowly. Staring unseeing at the lake in front of her, she tried to regain her control. He moved one hand downward until it rested low on her stomach. With inner despair she wondered if the entire romantic evening had been one big plot to get her right here.

Tair's hands stilled. He said softly, "Kate, upon my oath, I will not take you tonight. This is your fantasy. I give it freely. I ask only that you trust me enough to enjoy it fully. Can you do that for me?"

She tensed. It was a risk. Her brain spun as she tried to reason if she could really trust him enough to let go and not worry about the possible consequences. He had phenomenal self-control, but he could be playing some kind of deeper game to get her totally vulnerable. Then, he could press for intercourse. If she weakened and failed to resist, she'd be stuck here forever.

The thought wasn't as horrible as it had sounded days ago, but she felt scared. Trust him? No, she trusted herself, not someone else. It was hard to be fully confident of her ability to resist, though, when her body was screaming with need. Still, he had never broken oath with her. He had a deeply ingrained integrity that she admired. She felt torn.

She wished she knew what he was really feeling at this moment. She said suddenly, "I know you've been scanning, but merge with me. Right now."

There was silence for a moment. Even the sounds of the animals in the distance seemed to stop. Then, the quiet was broken when Tair vowed fiercely, "You will learn to trust me one day."

He merged with her suddenly, moving through her mind in one sure stroke. She trembled at the force of his feelings pouring through her. There was desire, so intense it made her breath catch. With that desire, there was tenderness, and anger or...hurt. She couldn't tell. The emotions were too strong.

However, one thing was clear. She knew with absolute certainty that he was telling the truth. His sincerity and desire for her to believe him were enormous. She relaxed and drew a shuddering breath. She said solemnly, "Thank you, Tair. I'm sorry. I trust you now."

He said simply, "I know."

With a quick movement, he hugged her body close, wrapping around her. He moved his hand low on her stomach. Avoiding her aching sex, he moved his hand downward over her hip and then her thigh. He reached the bottom of her skirt and said gently, "Relax, *sheka*. Live your fantasy. It is my gift to you."

She nodded her head and closed her eyes. Focusing on his hand at her breast and the other hand on her thigh, she could feel herself relaxing into the sensations. He moved his hand under her skirt along her inner thigh. The heat of it there made her tremble anew. She felt her muscles go lax as he traced upward in teasingly slow strokes.

His anticipation only added to her own. She could feel the pleasure he felt while touching her, and she trembled harder in response. The intensity was overwhelming.

Finally, his hand reached right below her sex and he paused. His voice was harsh, nearly guttural, "The knowledge that you have worn nothing under this skirt has been destroying me for hours."

She felt a thrill at his words. To know she affected this man so strongly made her feel powerfully female and desirable. She had no sooner acknowledged the feeling before his hand moved.

He cupped her sex and rubbed gently. She moaned. Her hands gripping the railing turned white from her grip. Tossing her head upward, she muttered, "Ahhh…that feels so good."

He pressed his palm against her clit. Her breath caught at the pressure as the pleasure spiked through her. She pressed forward into his hand.

The hand on her breast plucked her nipple and she struggled to keep from giving in to release.

He said huskily, "Not yet. Soon."

His palm moved away and he began teasing her with his fingers. He traced her lips with slow gentle movements, as if learning her for the first time. Moving slowly, up and down, he tormented her with that soft touch. It was too much.

Her mind blanked. She was captive to the needs of her body in a single instant. She was pushed further by the needs of his.

His fingers circled her clit and she moaned helplessly. She moved against those fingers, seeking more. He continued to stroke her, teasing her ruthlessly. The need for him pounded through her with every heartbeat. Her breath was coming in pants. She said, "Please..."

When she felt an answering thrust of one long finger into her sex, it rocked her. She could only whimper and shake. He probed inside her, stroking in and out slowly. She was slick and his finger slid forward and back easily, rasping sensitive nerve endings. She thought she heard a low curse, and then a second finger joined the first.

She felt the hard length of them fill her just as Tair moved forward and pressed his cock against her bottom. She gave a loud moan at the feel of his hardness against her ass. She wanted his cock inside her so much that she nearly begged. She wanted more. She needed it.

Tensing, she felt her sex clinch hard around his fingers. She lingered on the edge of release. The only thing separating his hard cock from her aching sex was a few thin layers of clothing. Images of him plunging inside her ran through her mind. His cock penetrating her aching sex, moving in powerful strokes. The feel of him inside her so hard and so big. She felt her body tightening. She wanted him. All of him. Nothing else mattered. It was so tempting. Maybe...

He froze and she could feel his indecision, the overwhelming temptation. His feelings of turmoil surged into her – triumph, guilt, desire, frustration, need. She couldn't separate one intense emotion fully from another as they rolled through her. Finally he muttered, "No! *Not* tonight. Come for me, Kate."

It was too much. At his denial, she went over the edge. Everything inside her went tight and then loose. The pulsing pleasure consumed her totally. She was completely lost to blind sensation. There was only the feel of his hard fingers stroking inside her, his hand on her breast, his cock against her ass, her sex clenching and relaxing. There was only pure pleasure.

When the last wave faded, she clung to the rail with renewed desperation. Her body felt limp. Her legs were still shaking. When Tair gave a sudden groan, she cried out in surprise.

His pleasure flooded through her, swamping her senses and making her scream. He groaned loudly as he found his own release. The two of them shook from the force of it, and then went still.

Kate came back to awareness slowly. The sounds of the animals in the night registered first. Then, she felt the cool breeze from the lake and the heat from Tair draped over her. He moved back slowly and stood up. She did the same.

She released the rail and noted with surprise that her hands were aching from where she'd gripped it so hard. She flexed them a couple of times as she turned around to face Tair. He was blocking her again.

When she caught sight of his face, she swallowed hard. He looked...she couldn't describe it. He looked shaken, as if he'd seen a ghost or had a tremendous scare. Just as quickly as she thought it, his face changed and he smiled. He reached forward and lifted her hand from her side.

Rubbing it softly between his own hands and soothing the ache, he brought it slowly to his mouth. Then he placed a kiss into her palm, and said simply, "Thank you for the gift."

Kate could only stare at him wordlessly and wonder why her heart felt too big within her chest.

Chapter 12

Kate woke up on her ninth day in Shimeria to an empty bed. She turned onto her back and stretched lazily. She felt a smile tug her lips and knew she was being ridiculous. She was not a morning person. She should be glowering and irritably wishing for coffee.

Instead, she felt surprisingly content. The last six days had been incredible. During the day, she and Tair had explored Shimeria. The friendship that had sprung up between them surprised her. And at night... She sighed and felt the familiar warmth steal through. At night, they had explored each other.

He was a good companion and an inventive, generous lover. They had refrained from controversial subjects like linking or leaving, and in the end had gotten along very well. He still goaded her with good-natured teasing, and she still responded by giving him a hard time.

However, there was an underlying easy affection to it all that was unfamiliar. She hadn't just landed on an unfamiliar planet. Nothing about their affair was familiar territory either.

He had blocked her a great deal. She wondered about it, but figured he was trying to keep the peace. He had been careful not to push her sexually either. Well, he had fulfilled *a lot* of fantasies, but he hadn't pushed for intercourse very hard.

They had walked a very fine line sexually to satisfy each other. The only problem for her was the absence of that final act only tantalized her all the more. Each time they came together and didn't have intercourse, the desire to go all the way only grew greater. She laughed inwardly as she realized she sounded like a teenager.

Still, the lack of aggression from Tair bothered her in some indefinable way. She had a nagging feeling that everything was too perfect. She was waiting for unhappiness to rear its ugly head. She was used to being happy on her own, but she wasn't used to having that feeling with someone else. She distrusted it instinctively.

Yet, the fantasy popped into her head at times. She had thought occasionally about staying on Shimeria with Tair. Like some kind of crazy dream, she imagined working and coming home to him every night. She knew the relationship was doomed, but the lure of trying to make it work was strong.

She had waited for the intensity between them to die down, and it had to some degree. The passion still burned hotly, but there was comfort and affection underneath it. Thinking back to all the broken relationships in her life, she realized she should be thankful that her time with Tair was limited to two weeks. Already the thought of leaving produced a hollow ache in her chest. She didn't want to imagine what it would feel like if they had several months or years together before a split.

Shrugging her grim thoughts aside, she resolved to enjoy the time she had with Tair. Kate Carson was no wimpy whiner. She grabbed hold of life and wrung it dry. Feeling the need to do something, anything, she wondered what to do with all this energy.

The image of Sharon filled her mind. Sharon would have said, "Kate, what you need is a plan." With a broad smile, Kate gave a mental nod of agreement. Maybe she would surprise Tair today with some new move. She was no circus performer, but she might be able to come up with something to shock the hell out of him.

Sitting up, she brushed her hair back off of her face and listened. She didn't hear Tair moving around anywhere or feel him. He was blocking her obviously. Still not hearing him, she decided he must have gone out. She headed for the bathroom, plotting and planning.

Later, after she showered, she realized she had forgotten to bring clothes into the bathroom. She glanced around. One of his shirts was hanging from a hook. She hesitated. She was alone. The no clothing rule applied only when he was around. Besides, it was really more of a form of sexual foreplay than a rule. She rolled her eyes a little at the two of them and grabbed the shirt. Shrugging into it, she padded down the hallway barefoot, humming softly to herself.

Spotting Tair in the living room in a chair, she halted in sudden surprise at his presence and the look on his face. He was staring at nothing, but the expression on his face was grim. He was wearing pants; but his chest was bare and he was bootless.

Clearing her throat, she walked into the room, and said, "Good Morning."

She felt a chill go through her when he turned to face her. His eyes were hard and he looked dangerous. His lips moved in a small smile, but it didn't reach his eyes. He said pleasantly, "Good Morning, Kate. Please come greet me properly."

He was sounding very Shimerian suddenly. Kate admired his grasp of slang, but noticed his English grew more formal when he was feeling angry or some other intense emotion. It was not a good sign.

Wondering what had caused this sudden mood, she walked over to him and gave him a cautious kiss on his mouth. His mouth moved under hers with lazy precision. She felt the warm glow of arousal and pulled back to look at his face again.

He was looking at her with naked hunger in his eyes. The intensity of the look startled her. Before she could comment, his expression changed and he smiled warmly, with casual intimacy.

Tumbling her onto his lap, he cradled her close and kissed her enthusiastically. When he raised his head, she looked up at him in surprise. She said huskily, "Well, good morning."

He grinned and said simply, "You look beautiful."

Kate felt heat rise into her face. It was ridiculous to be so touched by such a simple compliment and a few kisses and hugs. Lifting her chin, she said with mock solemnity, "Of course. It's a curse. Thousands of men throw themselves at my feet each day, but I endure."

Tair ran a finger down her cheek and laughed. Suddenly, he raised his head and a resigned look passed over his face. Kate asked, "What is it?"

Tair looked back down at her and asked, "Kate, do you trust me?"

Kate was uncomfortable at the sudden question. She did trust him on a lot of levels. In fact, she trusted him more than she should, given her track record and their current situation. She looked away and searched for an evasion. Her heart pounded as she really thought about his question.

Tair felt his heart sink when she made no response. The temptation to scan her thoughts was great, but he needed to hear the words. Just as he was sure that she was going to answer negatively or evade, he heard a soft-spoken, "yes" in the silence of the room. He lifted her chin and looked into her eyes. She looked miserable, but honest. It was enough.

Kate saw the relief flood Tair's face. He was acting so strangely this morning. What was his problem? She opened her mouth to ask when the front door opened.

With a sinking feeling, she watched Jadik stroll into the room. Her thoughts went into a frantic spin as she realized that the linking discussion had just gone to the top of the agenda. She straightened up and climbed off of Tair in a hurry.

Jadik said warmly, "Hello!"

Kate stood next to Tair's chair and sent looks back and forth to the two of them in silent accusation. Settling on Jadik as her first target, she said icily, "On my world it is common courtesy to knock."

Jadik looked confused at her words. Raising an eyebrow, he answered mildly, "I broadcast my coming arrival to Tair. He answered me. On my world that is considered courtesy enough."

Kate felt off-balance and extremely agitated. Without thinking, she said coolly, "Yes, well, I'm human, not Shimerian. A mental knock doesn't cut it. If you want to enter our home, you'll knock physically, too."

Suddenly realizing just how much she had revealed, she added, "I meant Tair's home. While I'm here." She turned and paced further away from the two of them.

Tair felt like shouting his triumph at her mistake. He was making more progress than he had thought. With more confidence, he said boldly, "Kate, you must link with Jadik today."

Looking at her with total sincerity, he said firmly, "Your protection supercedes all else."

Kate knew deep down that there was no way around it. She had gone over the tutorials during her brief times alone, looking for some loophole, but could find none. It was Shimerian law. He was a cop. She was an attorney and a law-abiding person, too. She had no desire to become a criminal at this point. She could even appreciate that it was a tradition and a safety measure that was old and ingrained.

She felt uneasy and unsure about it, but she understood their point of view. Buying time, she said coolly, "I haven't made my decision yet."

Jadik sat down in the chair across from Tair and watched her calmly. In a soothing voice, he said, "Kate, I may be able to help."

Kate regarded him suspiciously. She liked Jadik, but there was something about him that made her nervous. He reminded her of an iceberg. What you saw on the surface was only the tip. She asked shortly, "How?"

Tair watched their exchange and held his breath. If Jadik was going in the direction he suspected, the results could be positive or completely disastrous. With Kate, there was no way of knowing how she would react.

Jadik leaned forward and said calmly, "You do not trust me. It makes it difficult for you to feel comfortable."

Well, that was true. She didn't see what they could do about it, though. Nodding her head in agreement, she said, "No offense, Jadik, but I don't know you very well."

He nodded his understanding and said gravely, "To have trust, one must give it. I am going to reveal something to you that very few know. There are rumors about my abilities, but very few people know the extent of them. If they became common knowledge, my life would be in jeopardy. I would be treated as an oddity or even a threat. I am trusting you with my life now as I ask you to trust me."

Kate was extremely curious. Jadik was staring at her with total intensity and sincerity. The effect was pretty powerful. She gave a nod and said simply, "I won't tell anyone."

She walked to the sofa and sat down with her body angled toward him. She added gravely, "I promise."

Jadik gave her a slight smile and said, "First of all, I am a shifter."

Kate was confused. In a surprised voice, she said, "You're bisexual?"

He looked stunned and then repelled. When Tair burst into laughter, Jadik shot him a lethal glare. He said slowly and with great enunciation, "I am attracted to only women. That is not at all what I meant."

Kate couldn't help smiling at the indignant look on his face. It broke the gravity of the moment. Relaxing her shoulders, and leaning back on the sofa, she said, "Now, Jadik, it was a perfectly logical mistake. I have no idea what a shifter is."

Jadik still looked a little unsettled at her assumption, but he said, "I am a shapeshifter. You have probably seen some of the animals here with the same ability."

Kate was shocked. Recoiling at little, she ordered, "Tell me you don't turn into a rat."

Tair interrupted indignantly, "Deva is not a rodent. She is a *sheka*."

Kate rolled her eyes. "Whatever."

A sudden thought occurred to her. Looking at Jadik with horror, she exclaimed, "Oh, no! Tell me you're not...!"

Now Jadik rolled his eyes. The humor of it struck him and he asked teasingly, "Have you ever seen us in the same room together?"

Kate made a choking sound.

Jadik laughed uproariously. "I am joking. No, I am not Deva or any *sheka*."

She continued to regard him suspiciously. He became sober and said earnestly, "Kate, I vow to you I am not a rat or a rodent of any kind. Truly."

Turning to Tair, he said, "I cannot believe I have said those words."

Tair laughed until his sides ached. Kate would never cease to surprise him. There was no one like her. Only Kate could get one of the most powerful men on the planet to make such a ridiculous oath.

Kate believed him. They might think it was a bizarre suggestion, but she had been on Planet Kink long enough to know that things were often not what they seemed. Relieved, she asked, "Okay, then what do you change into?"

Jadik said, "I have different forms, but they are all Shimerian. In other words, they are merely different body forms I can assume at will."

When she arched an eyebrow and opened her mouth, he said quickly, "All of them are male forms. I am not female."

Jadik shot a suspicious look at Tair, but Tair was studying the ceiling as if in great thought. However, the smile tugging at the corners of his mouth gave away his true feelings.

Jadik glared at him and said, "You could help with explanations. She is your pactmate."

Tair gave up and laughed. He said, "Yes, Jadik, but you are handling it so well."

Kate asked, "You mean, you can look like someone else?"

Jadik turned back to her. "Yes, I have several different forms. The body size is approximately the same, but the individual features are different. I use the shifting in my work sometimes to hide my identity. It is effective."

Abruptly turning very serious, he said, "Kate, shifters are rare and not understood. Many people regard someone different as a threat. It is this way on your planet as well as mine."

He continued grimly, "However, I hide my ability for other reasons as well. There are certain mental abilities that come with the gift. I would rather not discuss them now, but I ask you to trust me. We will talk about them some time if you have questions. I will answer you honestly."

Kate nodded her head in agreement. The whole ability to shift was a strange idea and she figured her quota of bizarre was pretty much filled for the day. Staring at Jadik, she tried to picture him assuming another form the way Deva had in the bathroom. Somehow, she couldn't imagine it.

Jadik said, "My confession has two purposes, Kate. I want to prove that I trust you so that you will feel more comfortable. In addition, the ability to shift may make linking more acceptable." The last part of his statement was said in a carefully neutral tone.

Kate looked at Tair. He looked somber, although his expression was bland. Jadik looked just as blank faced and unexpressive. She asked curiously, "What does shifting have to do with linking?"

Jadik said, "You can pick which form you desire. I will link with you in that state."

Multiple Jadik's to choose from? The thought was scary as hell. With a grimace, Kate said, 'I believe I'll stick with the original."

A thought stuck her and she asked, "Is this the original?"

He smiled. "Yes, this is my natural form."

Leaning forward, he said softly, "Kate, you may pick another form that you desire more or desire less. Whatever will make you feel more comfortable with the sexuality of the link."

Kate was tempted for a second. Part of the reason she was so uncomfortable with the damn linking thing was her attraction to Jadik. In a sense, she was afraid that it would get out of hand. It would go only as far as the three of them wanted it to go. The problem was she was nervous about where her stopping point might be.

Still, picking a less desirable form felt almost cowardly. Almost like refusing to take a test out of fearing she'd fail it. It wasn't her style and it wasn't the way she wanted to live her life.

With sudden decision, she raised her chin and said, "When I link, I accept no substitutes or imitations."

Jadik sat back with relief and gave an amused smile at her phrasing. He had to admire her spirit. She was confused by the cultural differences, but she was facing them squarely.

Tair felt overwhelming relief and a sense of pride. She had studied their culture and understood what was at stake. She was facing her fears and battling her way through them in the most direct way.

Tair stood up and gave her a warm smile. Crossing to the couch, he paused and looked down at her. He said simply, "Thank you, Kate. Now, it is time to link."

Chapter 13

Kate realized several things simultaneously. First of all, she was wearing a shirt and nothing else. Granted, it was Tair's shirt, so it was very loose and came down to mid-thigh, but she was extremely conscious of her lack of panties. Secondly, she had just agreed to sexual activity with two men for the first time in her life. And she hadn't even had breakfast yet. Third, she was scared out of her mind.

Swallowing past the lump in her throat, she attempted to ask nonchalantly, "So, shouldn't we have a drink first or maybe throw on some mood music?"

What kind of music did you play in this situation? The theme from that very old classic Twilight Zone series filled her head. Appropriate, but not exactly the mood she was seeking. She gave a choked laugh in response.

Tair exchanged a look with Jadik and then held out his hand to her. He asked gently, "Kate?"

Kate looked at his hand and then looked into his face. It was now or never. She placed her hand in his and stood up on shaky legs.

Tossing her hair back, she said nervously, "There won't be any more surprises, right? You have just one form and I've seen it before. We're merely adding a new dimension to a familiar theme."

Tair enveloped her in a strong hug. She was vibrating with nerves. Placing a kiss to the top of her head, he said, "Kate, I will be scanning you the whole time. Nothing unacceptable or awful is going to happen. You have my oath. Please trust me."

His voice came out huskier than he intended as he added, "It will be extremely pleasurable."

When she clung to him without lifting her head, he cleared his throat and teased softly, "Kate Carson conquers planets. Two men are mere trifles."

Kate raised her head and lifted her chin. It was time she found her backbone. Pulling away from him, she said tartly, "Obviously, I'm going to have to take charge. The two of you are way too emotional about sex."

Both men lifted their eyebrows at her in disbelief, but she ignored them and strolled over to the bar. Tair had told her that he put the bar in just three weeks ago. It was long, running nearly the length of the room and not very tall, but fairly broad. It had a small food and drink transport accessible from the back. She stared blankly down at the dark top of it for a second in panic.

At the moment she was grateful he had installed it. She didn't really plan to have a drink at this hour, but she needed a distraction, any distraction. Her heart was pounding like a drum in her chest. She was going to have a heart attack.

Tair followed behind her. As they arrived at the bar, she was startled when he reached around her and planted both hands on it, caging her.

Spinning around within the circle of his arms, she stepped away from him until the bar bit into her back. Looking up, she said, "Yes?"

Tair leaned down and placed a gentle kiss on her mouth. He lifted his head before Kate could respond. His eyes had grown darker and his look was piercing.

His tone was pure temptation. "Kate, remember *Yginfa's*? How the fear intensified your arousal?"

The image of her orgasm flashed through her mind. The fear of discovery. The intensity of the pleasure. She felt the hum of arousal start through her body. She nodded.

Tair said, "This will be even better." He leaned down and gave her a hard kiss.

Kate reached up and caught his head in her hands. Running her fingers through his hair, she leaned into the kiss. Her mouth opened wide and she met his tongue with her own. As the velvet warmth of his tongue penetrated her mouth, she felt her nipples harden.

She stepped closer and leaned against the hard length of his body. When the sensitive tips of her breasts pressed against his chest through the thin shirt, she nearly moaned in relief. She felt his arms come around her and stroke down her back.

She arched further into him as the kiss grew hotter. His hands moved downward and clasped her butt. As his fingers gripped and relaxed in a familiar rhythm, her sex ached in direct response.

Suddenly, he picked her up and sat her on the top of the bar. She was startled and grabbed his shoulders for balance. He moved between her thighs and pulled her forward at the same instant. Her sex came into contact with his hard cock and she moaned at the pure pleasure of it.

He felt huge and throbbing. His pants were the only barrier between them. With aching frustration, she yearned to feel his naked cock plunging into her. It was a familiar feeling.

The restraint they had exercised in the past days haunted her with a vengeance. She wanted him inside her with a need that rocked her soul. Leaning back on her hands, she arched upward and pressed against his cock harder.

Tair moaned and tried to hold onto control desperately. Kate was pushing him to the edge with her thoughts. Her nipples stood out in defiance against the thin material of his shirt.

Her sex was wet and pressing against him. He could feel the heat of her through his pants and it was making him crazy. He wanted to pump into her until she screamed.

As they moved against each other in an echo of the act they both craved, he sent a silent call to Jadik. It was time. Things were rapidly getting out of control.

Kate was conscious of Jadik, but he wasn't in her line of vision, so she had pushed the thought of him to the back of her mind. As she had become lost in Tair, she had forgotten him further. The aching pleasure of her body and the feel of Tair had consumed her.

With a sense of shock, she heard Jadik's husky voice from across the room. He ordered firmly, "Kate, you need to slow down. We have much to explore."

She went rigid with surprise at his tone. The power and arrogance behind it annoyed her, but it was strangely arousing, too. She sat up and glared at him over Tair's shoulder.

In response, he stared hard at her and began unbuttoning his shirt with slow movements. When he shrugged the shirt off and tossed it over the chair, her heart leapt into her throat. All of that long dark hair fell down onto well-defined shoulders. His chest was muscular with a dark shadow of hair. That shadow led downward to the top of his pants. She swallowed hard.

Tair felt his control returning and cursed himself silently. Kate could get to him as no other. The days of denial only added to the strain. The link was too important. He had to focus and remain in control.

Taking a step back from her, he nearly moaned at the loss of contact. He took a few deep breaths and then moved to the far end of the bar. He said huskily, "Come here."

Kate complied without thinking. Her body was on fire and her thoughts were scattered. She scooted across the bar in awkward movements and faced him. He pulled her legs forward until she was on the very edge of the bar.

Taking her thighs in his hands, he pulled them apart and then leaned down to place a soft kiss on the inside of each knee. He put first one leg, and then the other over his shoulders.

Kate leaned back on her hands as she felt a shiver run through her. Tair was teasing her with soft kisses and gentle licks along the inside of her lower thighs. As she watched his dark head move between her legs, she swallowed a moan.

She felt Jadik walking across the room, but ignored him. He reached the side of the bar next to her and she became very conscious suddenly of his body leaning close.

She felt his hand under her chin as he turned her head toward him and up. Looking into his face, she saw he was gazing at her mouth with heavy-lidded intensity. He brought his mouth down firmly in a tongue-thrusting kiss. There was no gentle patience or teasing temptation to the kiss. He took her mouth and demanded a response.

Kate could feel Tair's kisses along her thighs climbing higher. It was too much. The contrast between his teasing caresses and Jadik's force was too much. With a moan, she began kissing Jadik back. Her mind was reeling and her body was out of control.

Jadik broke the kiss and pressed his mouth hard to her neck. As he licked and bit along the side of it, she moved her head and gave in to the pleasure. His hands came up to her shoulders and he pushed her backward gently.

She could feel the cool length of the bar through the shirt against her back as she laid down. Jadik leaned over her and ran one finger along the edge of the shirt across the tops of her breasts. Her nipples ached and her hands balled into fists at the teasing touch.

Tair's hands moved to the hemline of the shirt. He pushed the shirt up a few inches and continued to tease. The velvet wetness of his tongue scraped along her inner thighs in maddeningly slow movements. As his kisses continued upward, he raised her hemline higher and higher, inch-by-inch. It was pure sensual torture.

Jadik's hand went to the top button on her shirt. He asked softly, "How many buttons will you allow me to open, hmmm?"

With a quick flick, the first button came undone. She felt him run the rough backs of his fingers along her skin at the top of the shirt. His fingers traveled over more of her as the top of the shirt opened a little wider. As he traced the top of her breasts, she felt the shirt catch on her sensitive nipples. She sucked in a breath.

Jadik asked slowly, "Feeling out of control, Kate? How far will we go?"

His hand reached the next button and flicked it open. The back of his fingers wandered into the valley between her breasts and traced the curves there. She swallowed a moan.

Kate felt cool air as Tair raised the hemline up to her stomach. His head hovered over her sex. She felt his breath as he blew softly into her curls and said in a rough voice, "No mercy until you scream, *sheka*."

The wet heat of his tongue licked into her sex. She whimpered. She felt the vibration of his mouth against her mound as Tair said, "You will have to do better than that." He circled her clit with teasing swirls and then sucked gently.

Kate felt heat run through her body like fire. The feel of Tair's tongue and mouth was too much. She arched her hips upward to get closer to that delicious torment. She started to move her upper body weight up onto her elbows.

Jadik grabbed her hands before she was able to get up. In one quick move, he pulled them over her head. Grasping her wrists in the warm strength of one big hand, he leaned down close to her face and chuckled, "No."

Watching her eyes, he said huskily, "Where was I? Oh, yes, I believe I was opening your shirt." He brought his free hand down until he reached the third button.

Kate pushed her wrists against his grip, but it remained firm. He wasn't hurting her. She was scared, but too aroused to say no.

Jadik flicked the button through the loop with casual efficiency. Then he ran his hand in one long stroke from her neck all the way down to between her breasts. She trembled. He smiled, still holding her gaze. Then he looked down and watched as he moved his hand against the edge of the shirt and swept it to one side.

She felt cool air wash over her exposed breast. She held her breath. The wait seemed endless. Finally, he swept the other side of the shirt away, leaving both breasts exposed and then paused. Kate felt like she was going out of her mind.

Tair was tormenting her sex with delicate precision. He knew exactly how to touch her with his mouth and tongue. He was playing her the way a musician plays an instrument that he loves – with total familiarity, absorption, and skill. His tongue teased and tormented her clit exactly the way that she liked. It was incredibly maddening and intensely pleasurable.

She could feel Jadik's gaze as he stared at her breasts. She could feel the cool air in direct contrast to the heat of his gaze. The need for release was riding her hard. She wanted to come. She let out a moan of frustration and need.

She watched as Jadik leaned down and began placing wet kisses in circles over her breast around her aching nipple, without actually touching it. She whimpered, "It's too much."

Jadik paused. She could feel the heat of his breath over her nipple as he muttered huskily, "It can never be too much."

He captured her nipple in his mouth and sucked hard. His fingers curled around her other nipple and gently pinched. The feel of that dual tugging sent her to the edge.

Suddenly, Kate felt the hard thrust of Tair's fingers probing the inner walls of her sex. She cried out and felt tears of frustration spring to her eyes. She could feel his mouth against her clit as he ordered, "Let go. Give in to it now. Take your pleasure."

Tair circled her clit with his tongue and then sucked. His fingers thrust into her and upward, and he pressed hard against that sensitive spot inside her.

Then suddenly, he thrust even harder into her mind. His desire and pleasure swept through her like wildfire. She felt her entire body go rigid and her breath caught.

Her sex clenched and then pleasure exploded inside her like a bomb. She screamed as wave after wave swept through her. There was no thought, no world beyond the pure pleasure of her body's release.

Tair moaned and clung desperately to control. He concentrated hard and tried to work quickly with Jadik to get the link into place. He knew Kate's pleasure had both of them suspended in complete agony on the edge.

Jadik leaned down, laying across Kate, feeling her hard nipples stab into his chest. He felt sweat break out on his forehead as he mentally built the link. As Kate's screams died away, the link was completed. It was done. He began to lift upward and away from her body. The aching pain of his cock made his movements slow.

Tair raised his head, removed her legs from his shoulders, and slowly stood. It hurt to move. He gazed helplessly at Kate, caught by the vision of her in that moment. She was lying sprawled against the bar in total abandon. Her body was flushed with the shirt bunched around her middle. Her breasts and sex were exposed.

The hard points of her nipples, usually pink, were very red and still glistening. Her sex was red, too, swollen and wet. His hands went to the top of his pants in an instinctive move to strip them off and plunge inside her.

Kate could feel Tair's intent. She felt dreamy and floating, drunk from the intensity of her release. Sitting up with slow languorous movements, she looked from one man to the other.

She could see that Jadik was sweating, his big body tense and dangerously on edge. Tair's hands had stopped at the top of his pants, but it was obvious to her what it was costing him. She sat up completely and looked into his face. His eyes were stark with naked hunger and the frustration of a predator denied the kill at the last second.

She looked over her shoulder at Jadik, standing silently on the other side of the bar. In a husky voice, she ordered, "Jadik, open the link and share my thoughts."

Turning to Tair, she demanded, "Stay merged with me."

Both Tair and Jadik froze at her words. She let her imagination run wild with graphic images. She pictured the three of them in the bedroom lying on the bed with her in the middle.

Tair was on his side, plunging his hard cock inside her wet sex in long, hard strokes as she faced him on her side. She pictured Jadik's big body lying behind her. She imagined the feel of his cock as it moved in her ass with those same long strokes.

She pictured the two of them stroking in and out in slow controlled movements, gradually building speed. And she imagined in glorious, vivid detail exactly how it would feel. The hardness. The fullness. The slick slide of all three of their bodies. The incredible pleasure.

Reaching forward, Kate opened the button on Tair's pants, then another and another. His cock sprang free, huge and visibly throbbing. She took it in her hand in one long, firm, slow stroke. Moving upward, still flooding them both with images, she gave him another firm stroke and then another, timed exactly with the image in her mind. He was breathing heavily, but his breath caught in his throat.

In one agonized moan, he went over the edge. She could feel the pulsing of his cock in her hand and felt his warm wetness slide over her fist. His pleasure swamped her and she threw back her head in response. It felt incredible, beyond good.

Jadik gripped the edge of the bar hard. Kate's images were making him crazy with need. It was too much. He lost control and felt his cock throb as pulse after pulse of pleasure stole his breath. Release came with an intensity that blanked his mind and stole his strength.

Kate lowered her head and looked at the two men. Both of them were gripping the counter like it was a lifeline. Their heads were down and she watched them with sleepy appreciation. Suddenly, both men raised their heads and stared at her intently. She wondered what they were thinking.

Jadik was thinking that Kate was an extraordinary woman. Tair had found a pactmate of strength, beauty, and passion.

Tair was thinking one simple thought. "Hell-on-wheels."

Chapter 14

The next day started out with a comfortable sense of normalcy. Kate was surprised at how she was feeling. The linking the day before had been erotic and intense, but it had felt very natural, too. The gap between Earth and Shimerian cultures had been a wide one, but she felt like they had bridged it.

She knew she ought to feel weird about the whole thing, but she didn't. She supposed it had to do with her trust in Tair and even Jadik to a certain degree. She felt good.

Tair was sitting on the couch beside her, one big arm wrapped around her. They had just eaten "midmeal" and were relaxing, talking about the sights they had seen in the last few days. Tair was absently playing with her hair in a familiar gesture. The man was forever touching her and cuddling her. Kate frowned inwardly when she realized just how used to that touching she had become.

Glancing at Tair, she asked, "Are we going somewhere today?"

Tair turned and looked at her. He drawled teasingly, "I had no plan for today. We will have to explore what it is you desire most."

She arched an eyebrow at his phrasing and smiled. Any response left her head at the sudden look of alarm that crossed his face. His entire body went rigid and he brought his hand to his head in reflex. A look of agony and pain spread over his features.

Kate felt the first wave of intense shock and dread radiate from him and caught her breath. She demanded, "What is it?"

Tair threw up a mental block as big and hard as he could in two directions. Their merge would only magnify the shock, his feelings heightening her own. He had to protect Kate. On the heels of that thought, he knew it was impossible. He looked at her concerned face and felt dread all the way to his soul.

Kate felt his block and the emotional waves stopped abruptly. What the hell was happening? Tair had gone pale. Feeling impatient and worried beyond belief, she demanded, "What the hell is going on, Tair?"

Tair stared into her face and searched for words. Finally, he said gently, "Kate, I am Sharon's link. She is okay, but she is in intense emotional pain. Liken is with her."

Kate felt the blood drain from her face. She asked, "Has she been hurt? What happened?"

Tair said gently, "She is physically well. Kate, it is Gage."

Kate heard his words, but shook her head in denial. She jumped up from the couch and paced a few feet away. Tair was watching her with obvious compassion and a look of profound worry. She denied flatly, "You're wrong."

Tair stood up and walked to her. Placing gentle hands on her shoulders he said, "Kate, there was an accident. His heart stopped during emergency transport. They are trying to revive him, but it has not worked yet."

Kate broke away from him and turned her back. This couldn't be happening. Gage was fine. It was a bad dream. He couldn't be gone.

She thought of his last words to her at the pact ceremony and knew with sudden certainty that he had been saying goodbye. He had known.

She felt pain cut through to her soul. It was beyond bearing. The physical shock of it nearly drove her to her knees. Her breath hitched and she couldn't breath. She felt a voice from deep within scream and scream.

Then, a welcome numbness stole over her, like a blanketing fog. She felt nothing. Nothing at all. She took a deep breath and let it out slowly.

Turning to face Tair, she said calmly, "I'm going to put on some clothes and get ready to go."

He looked at her helplessly. She walked out of the room.

Tair sent a mental message to Liken of concern and paced the room with agitation. He couldn't stand it. She was in so much pain. He felt his heart twist again in agony as he remembered the look on her face when she believed him. He had to do something. He had to help her. He had to find a way. He heard Jadik's call just as the front door opened.

Jadik burst into the room, out-of-breath, and demanded, "Where is she?"

Tair tried to gather his composure. He said, "My apologies. I should have explained. I could think only of what she was feeling. I forgot that you would receive her thoughts. I should have sent you an explanation."

Jadik shrugged the apology off, and demanded, "Take care of her! Fix it!"

Tair repeated in the same tone, "Fix it?"

Jadik paced. He was disturbed and worried. "She is in shock. She is in extreme pain. She cannot continue this way."

Tair nodded in agreement but said with frustration, "There is no fixing it. She has lost her brother."

He felt furious at his inability to help her. His heart ached in his chest at the thought of her pain. He felt an unfamiliar helplessness pressing in on him. He grabbed his shirt from the couch and shrugged into it. Then, he leaned down and put on his boots with angry, jerky movements.

Jadik looked tired suddenly. He said apologetically, "I know, Tair. I am sorry. This is very disturbing. She is hurting. I know you would change it if you could."

Kate appeared in the doorway. Her face was white, and her body was unnaturally rigid. She said tonelessly, "We need to go back now. I'm ready. Take me back."

Tair moved to her and placed a gentle arm around her shoulders. He said, "Kate, they are working on him. There is still hope."

She raised lifeless eyes to his and said, "I want to see him now."

Tair said gently, "Okay, then we will go."

Jadik said suddenly, "Tair, what if..."

Tair silenced him with a single look.

Understanding washed through Jadik, and he said quietly, "Let's go."

Chapter 15

Kate was wrapped and existing in a world of childhood memory. She was conscious of the two men by her side during the trip back to Earth, but she fought to keep the reality of their presence from her mind. She was with Gage, instead, in the past.

Gage was tugging her ponytail, teasing her. His teenaged body was lanky and he was all arms and legs. His blue eyes were lit with laughter as he chided, "Kit-Kate, you don't know the first thing about men."

She turned all of her teenage indignation in his direction. With a furious glare, she said, "He's wonderful. A total landmark."

Gage raised a skeptical eyebrow and mocked, "Landmark?"

She gave a derisive sniff at his usual and deliberate ignorance of teenage slang. He thought he was too old for it. He was a "man" now. "Yes, landmark – well-built and worth studying."

She gave him an impish smile, "The kind of sight that makes you want to come again and again."

Gage gave her a disgusted glare. She said haughtily, "What do you know? You're not a man. You're a toad."

Then, Gage sitting next to her on the steps of the old house, the two of them silent in the eerie moonlight. He was saying quietly, "Kate, he's not worth it. Not worth one of your tears. I'll kill him and be done with it. Just say the word."

Turning to look at him, her young heart broken, but soothed by his words, she said, "Thanks, Gage, but I think we have to let him live."

She wiped the tears from her face, and sniffed, straightening her shoulders. Then she smiled with sudden weak humor. "But that doesn't mean he has to live happily. I have a plan…"

In the living room, late at night, the two of them were talking. Gage, his eyes sad and wistful, his face pale and looking grim, saying, "Kate, I hate it. It's not a gift but a curse."

The comfortable feel of her brother as she wrapped her arms around his body and held him tight. The warmth as his arms came around her and he wept silent, bitter tears. Feeling tears of her own slide hot and wet from her eyes at his pain.

The memories flooded her mind. Each more precious than the next. The two of them laughing, fighting, and teasing in an endless kaleidoscope of love. Her brother, Gage. Gage.

Tair spoke next to her ear, "Kate, we are here."

Kate knew she had to respond. His voice was insistent and worried. She looked around and realized with shock that they were at the health building. Suddenly noticing the bright lights and the bustling activity, she demanded, "Where is he?"

Tair left out a breath of relief. She was responding. Her withdrawal had terrified him. She had allowed him and Jadik to take her back with total docility.

At the Pactbuilding, she had remained standing, completely silent as he briefly left her with Jadik to talk with Pactofficials. Even going through the portal, she had barely blinked. It was killing him. He couldn't stand to see her this way.

Kate saw Sharon coming down the corridor toward them. When Sharon spotted her, she stopped dead and then came running forward. Wrapping her arms around Kate, she said desperately next to her ear, "They've gotten him back and lost him twice. It will be a while before we know for sure. Kate, he can't die."

Kate pulled back and saw tears flooding down Sharon's cheeks. In a quiet tone, Kate said, "Sharon, please don't cry. I can't handle it."

Sharon studied her face silently. Bringing her hands up to swipe the tears off her cheeks, she said, "I'm sorry. I'm sure you're right. He'll be just fine. Crying won't help."

That wasn't what Kate meant, but she couldn't stand the sight of those tears on Sharon's cheeks. They threatened to pull her from the safety of her numbness and drag her into a world where feeling existed.

Liken strode down the corridor with two coffees in his hand. Handing one to Sharon and the other to Kate, he ordered firmly, "Drink."

Kate drank, barely aware of the hot liquid as it made its way down her throat. Liken flashed a worried look to Tair in silent question. Tair shook his head and wrapped an arm around Kate.

Pulling her gently, he led her over to a group of chairs. He guided her into one and sat down next to her, keeping her close within the circle of his arms. She felt so small against him. He forgot sometimes with that huge spirit just how small she really was.

Kate heard Sharon explaining the details of the accident to everyone. Gage had swerved to avoid another transport and struck a wall. His quick reflexes had saved the lives of the family in the other vehicle. The shaken father, whose attention had been preoccupied with one of the children in the back, had been overwhelmed and guilt-stricken at the accident.

The health center had tried to reach Kate, but upon finding out she was off-planet, had contacted Sharon next. In a strange twist, without Shimerian technology, he would not have survived even this long.

A health engineer stepped out from one of the rooms and made his way to them. Looking at the solemn group gathered, he asked, "Which one of you is Kate?"

Kate heard the words and responded to her name instinctively. She looked up and said, "Me."

He smiled kindly and said gently, "Your brother is quite a fighter. We lost him repeatedly, but he kept coming back. We have him stabilized and in a room now. We'll need to keep him for a while, but he should be fine in the long run."

As the health engineer kept talking, Kate heard the words, but couldn't understand the meanings. She knew at some level he was detailing Gage's injuries and what had been done to save him. But, the phrase that kept echoing through her mind was, "He should be fine."

She said suddenly, "I need to see him. Where is he?"

The health engineer looked surprised at her fierce tone, but responded kindly, "Room 1207. You may see him, but only for a minute. He's been asking for you."

Turning to the rest of the group, he said, "Sorry, but only one visitor for now."

Sharon was crying again, wrapped in a grinning Liken's arms. Tair wrapped his arms around Kate from behind and gave her a hard squeeze. Everyone was grinning in relief except Kate. Kate wanted to see her brother and she wanted to see him now.

Breaking out of Tair's arms and away from the group, she walked down the hallway, reading the numbers on the rooms as she went. Reaching Room 1207 she opened the door, and walked in silently.

She stopped abruptly as she saw the bed and all the equipment around it. Seeing Gage lying on it looking pale and still, she said his name in a broken voice, "Gage."

He turned his head and opened weary blue eyes. Smiling wanly, he said in a very shaky voice, "Died young and lived to tell the tale... How about that, Kit-Kate?"

Kate felt the world spin and grabbed the wall for support. Finally, raising her head, she said fiercely, "Don't you ever do that again! You and your stupid visions! You scared me to death!"

Rushing over to the bed, she knelt down and grabbed his hand. She kissed it and placed her forehead against it, silently giving thanks. The living warmth of his hand seeped into her own cold hand as she gave up trying to speak anymore.

Gage grimaced in pain as felt his sister clinging to his hand like a lifeline. He had died tonight. He had fought it and lost and come back to fight again. The sheer miracle of it ran through his veins like a drug. He had known his entire life that he would die young. And he had.

The nightmarish crash flashed through his mind again with remarkable clarity. The overwhelming pain and sense of coldness spreading through his body. The absolute feeling of certainty that he was dying. The fierce look on the emergency transport worker's face as he said, "We're losing him!" It was exactly as he had seen in his dreams and visions.

Now, as new possibilities stretched out before him, he felt a sense of awe and gratitude at the thought of a second chance. Feeling Kate's cold hand holding his tightly, he gave silent thanks once again.

Kate pulled back and said, "I love you, Gage."

He managed a rather weak grin and said, "Love you, too."

The health engineer walked in and said mock sternly, "You scared this poor young woman to death. It may take a long while to make it up to her."

Gage promised softly, "I plan to. I have time now." Placing his hand over hers on the bed, he said, "Plenty of time."

Chapter 16

Jadik was walking through the corridors of the health building, anxious to leave. It had been quite a day. He was grateful that everyone was fine, but the emotion of the events had shaken him.

He was a loner. He had friends, like Tair and Liken and even a few others, but he was used to staying on the edges of other people' lives. The feelings of worry and helplessness were new to him. That feeling of family was surprising as well. His own family was...he banished the thought.

It was all very confusing. With a mental shrug, he decided this pactmate business was complicated. When he found his own pactmate, he would proceed with care. In the meantime, he needed a new mission to distract him. Something that would be challenging and consuming.

He felt a slight, delicate touch mentally, like a gentle sad caress. Suddenly, realizing what was happening, he threw up a mental shield and glanced around. It had been close.

Scanning the people around him, he could read nothing out of the ordinary. Something was not right. He focused and sent out a much stronger probe. Immediately, he reached her mind. A name and a face popped into his head. An instant sense of recognition and rightness followed. The shock was so great that he froze in absolute disbelief.

Focusing harder, he reached out and brushed her mind again. When he felt a shield go up, he withdrew immediately, but it was enough. Turning on his heel, he walked back the way he had come until he reached a small waiting room. He stood in the doorway as his heart raced in his chest. He had found her. At last.

She was seated on a chair. Her head was bent down as she gazed at the floor. She had beautiful, wavy, golden-red hair down to her shoulders. At the moment, it was falling forward over her face, revealing the slender curve of her neck. She was incredibly petite, maybe 5"3' with a slender body that looked graceful and fragile. Sensing his presence, her head came up with a snap.

He knew that face and felt his breath catch in his throat. Her delicate features were covered with golden freckles. She had big brown eyes, which were presently brimming with tears. Jadik felt his chest tighten in response.

Her full mouth was drawn into a frown, which grew worse as she studied him silently. Finally, she said simply, "Jadik."

Just hearing his name in that husky voice, he felt the fierce tug of arousal. She was beautiful, and sweetly sexy, and he had found her. He walked forward and squatted in front of her so that they were face-to-face. In his most gentle voice, he said, "Hello, Cass."

Those big eyes widened slightly at his use of her nickname, but she blinked back her tears and said firmly, "Don't do it."

Startled, he asked, "What should I not do?"

She said solemnly, "Call me to Oath. I don't want a pactmate or a pledgemate. I'm human and I'm staying on Earth."

Jadik raised an eyebrow. She was confusing him. He needed to proceed with care. "You are only half-human. You are half-Shimerian, too."

Cass was trying to control her reaction. She couldn't believe he was here. She had been so careful for so many years. Confronted with his big body so close to her own, she felt the pull of their attraction with a sinking heart.

If she hadn't been so upset, he never would have located her. She cursed inwardly and tried to think. "Yes, my father is Shimerian and my mother is human. I was raised on Shimeria, but since I'm half-human I have been able to adapt. I'm not going back. I'm staying here."

Jadik said carefully, "You are on the register. It is required of all dual planet females."

She nodded resentfully and said fiercely, 'Of course. That means it's up to you to walk away. Don't summon me, Jadik. I mean what I say. I won't stay in Shimeria. I won't be your pledgemate. You'll regret it if you call me to Oath."

Jadik felt a smile tug at his lips. She sounded so fierce. It was rather humorous coming from such a small, delicate creature. He wondered if she really thought she could intimidate him.

Giving in to his amusement at her threat, he grinned at her. "Cass, I will call you soon. There is no need for this discussion. We will be happy together on Shimeria. You worry needlessly."

He stood and held out his hand. He thought he saw a brief flash of rebellion cross her face. He was somewhat surprised when she took it. Her small hand was soft and cold. She stood and took a sudden step forward, bringing her small body against his.

In an instant, his cock leapt to life. He was hard and throbbing. He looked down into her big brown eyes and felt a drowning sensation. He watched as she moistened her lips with a nervous tongue.

Giving in to temptation, he bent down and brushed his lips over hers. She responded immediately. He dipped his tongue along the seam of her mouth.

She opened her lips, and he thrust his tongue inward to explore. With a groan, he plundered and reveled in the taste and feel of her. When he felt her leg come up and wrap around the outside of his leg, he thought she was trying to get closer. It was a mistake that cost him dearly.

Cass swept the back of Jadik's knee with her foot in one quick decisive motion, while pushing hard with her hands against his chest. He was caught completely off guard, just as she had planned.

He reached out instinctively, but she stepped back just in time. He went down, arms flailing wildly, and landed awkwardly on his butt on the floor with an incredibly loud thump.

Stepping around and looking down at him, she said flatly, "Call me to Oath and I'll run. You won't find me. I'm good. I have my own Shimerian abilities. And as you can tell, I'm a lot meaner than I look."

She viewed his total astonishment with a great deal of pleasure and said smugly, "While you nurse that sore ass, I suggest you re-think your future. Mine's already set. And you're not a part of it." She walked toward the doorway of the room, immensely pleased with her exit line.

As she reached the doorway, he said from the floor, "Cass?"

She paused and looked back, arching an eyebrow in question.

Jadik grinned widely. "I will see you soon."

He was impossible. Cass rolled her eyes and said tartly, "Not if I see you first."

And she was gone. Jadik threw back his head and roared with laughter. She was indeed much meaner than she looked. Standing up with a wince, he rubbed his aching butt. She was surprising, but then again, he had a few surprises of his own. As he walked out of the door, he muttered, "We will see who re-thinks the future." Capturing Cass had become his new mission.

Chapter 17

Tair stared out the window of Kate's apartment, waiting for her to emerge from her bathroom. She had barely spoken, even after seeing her brother. The health engineer had escorted her from the room and explained that Gage would be fine. He needed to rest and to heal. The best thing Kate could do for him was to go home and visit the next night.

Liken and Sharon had dropped them at Kate's apartment, looking at Kate with worried faces and sending significant looks Tair's way. He knew what he had to do. He had to break through Kate's defensive shell. He knew what it would cost for both of them as well. He waited in dread and stared with unseeing eyes, listening for the sound of her footsteps.

Kate felt numb. The fog seemed to have lifted, but she had no sense of emotion at all. She felt completely removed from herself. Her apartment felt strange...and alien.

She had walked in and headed straight for the shower. She had stood silently under it, wondering if she would cry, but she hadn't. Feeling the water on her body, she noticed it felt strangely wet and thin. Nothing felt right. And she felt nothing.

She put on her clothes with mechanical movements before realizing she had put on her sandals, too. She didn't need to wear shoes in her apartment. Uncaring and not having the energy to remove them, she left them on and wandered out into the living room. Tair was by the window looking out. When he turned to face her, he looked grim.

He said firmly, "Kate, you cannot continue this way."

Kate felt a lump in her throat, but swallowed and said quickly, "I'm fine. I think I'll take a walk."

Tair walked until he stood directly in front of her. Staring at her with hard eyes, he said, "No."

She asked dully, "Why not?"

He placed both hands on her shoulders and said, "You will cease this running immediately. Kate Carson is not a coward."

She felt the first stirrings of surprise. She denied, "I'm not a coward. I'm going for a walk."

Tightening his grip, he said, "You are doing anything to avoid dealing with what has happened tonight. I will not allow it."

Kate tried to pull away, but he held firm. She said, "Gage is fine. I'm fine. There's nothing to deal with."

Tair challenged, "Then you do not need to walk, do you?"

When she pulled back this time, he let her go. She turned her back to him.

He said conversationally, "You never talk about your parents."

Kate spun around and said coldly, "I have no parents."

Tair gave her a half-smile. He said, "I do not believe that you were hatched."

He sobered and said quietly, "Your father died before you were born. Your mother abandoned you when you were eight years old.'

Kate turned away from him again and said coldly, "I don't think I need a history lesson."

He continued, "You and Gage were left with your aunt. A nice enough woman but one who had little time for children. That left only you and Gage to care for one another."

Kate could feel the words pressing in on her like a giant fist. She ordered icily, "Stop."

He said quietly, "No. You nearly lost him tonight. Your father, your mother. They left you, and then Gage nearly left you, too. How does it *feel*, Kate?"

Kate felt her breath hitch. That moment when Tair had told her about Gage flashed through her mind. She tried to push it away, but it stayed. She said brokenly, "You bastard."

Tair walked to her and put his hands on her shoulders from behind. Leaning down next to her ear, he said gently, "Kate, let go. No more hiding. I promise you. It is okay."

Feelings too big for her body rushed through her with the force of a hurricane. The fear, the pain, the helplessness, the horror, the anger, even the joy and relief, all of it built until she thought her chest would explode. Spinning around, she slammed both hands into his chest and yelled, "Stop it! Stop it right now!"

She was blinded by tears and hitting his chest weakly. Tair wrapped his arms around her and held her fiercely. Kate felt the last ounce of control break away, and with a moan of anguish, she let go and sobbed. Shudders wracked her body and she was crying so hard that she could barely breathe.

Tair picked her up and carried her to the couch. Sitting down, he cradled her in his lap and held her as she cried against his chest. Stroking her back with soothing motions, his own eyes misty, he said softly, "I am here, Kate. I am here. Everything will be fine." He placed gentle kisses into her hair and murmured softly in his own language.

Kate cried until she felt hollowed out inside. Her entire world had narrowed to the anguish of her feelings and the warmth and comfort of Tair's big body encircling her. Finally, her crying lessened and she regained some control.

Pulling back from his chest a little, she said softly, "I'm sorry. Your shirt is soaked."

Tair placed a gentle hand under her chin and raised her face. With great tenderness, he said, "I do not care about the shirt. I care only about you."

Kate gave him a weak smile and sniffed. He placed a gentle kiss on her forehead and sighed. "You scared me, Kate. Do not shut me out again. I may be able to scan your thoughts, but I have to block you when intense negative emotion is involved. You were so unresponsive, I was very worried."

Kate noticed for the first time how tired he looked. There were lines of weariness and strain in his face. He had been worried about her. The hollow feeling inside her began to fill with warmth. Raising her hand, she placed it on his cheek and said, "Thank you, Tair. I mean it. I'm sorry I called you a bastard."

He chuckled. With a teasing light in his eyes, he said, "I was being one at the time. Although I had a good reason. It is a hidden ability of mine."

She took her hand off his cheek and punched his chest lightly. She said, "Well, you are excellent at it, just like everything else."

At the mention of "everything else," the air became charged. Kate was very aware suddenly that she was on his lap. Her hand resting against his chest moved in an unconscious caress. She knew she looked like hell, but she didn't care. She wanted to be close to him. Leaning forward, she placed a gentle kiss on his mouth.

Tair watched the changing expressions on Kate's face in sudden awareness. She was looking at him so warmly without defenses or games. When she placed her mouth against his own, he responded, lightly moving his lips under her own. It was a kiss unlike any other they had shared -- the simple touching of lips, with pure tender feeling behind it.

Kate pulled back from the kiss and stared at him silently. Neither of them spoke. Finally, giving in to temptation, she moved forward and captured his mouth again.

This time, there was hunger and need in the kiss. She ran her tongue along the seam of his lips and felt them open. She raised her hands to his face and darted her tongue inside his mouth to explore. The feel of him, the taste of him was wonderful and familiar. She wanted more. She thrust harder into his mouth and the kiss caught fire.

Tair moaned and thrust back with hungry greed. She was kissing him passionately, no holding back. With every eager movement of her mouth, she communicated naked need. It was intoxicating and overwhelming, and it flayed him alive. He wanted more.

Kate pulled away and shifted in his lap until she was straddling him. Bringing her aching sex down onto his hard cock, she moaned as pleasure shot through her. Rubbing harder, she cursed the clothes separating them. Tair's arms came around her and he arched upward, increasing the pressure. Kate whimpered and her head fell back.

Tair fought for control. She was driving him crazy. The feel of her sex against his cock was pure temptation. He wanted to take her with every thing that was inside him. She lifted up suddenly and he nearly begged. Her hands went to the top button of his pants and he froze.

Kate was past caring about anything. She wanted him inside her no matter what it meant, no matter the consequences. She unbuttoned his pants with quick movements. His cock sprang into her hand, the smooth skin as soft as velvet. She wrapped her fingers around it and felt that hard length of it throb against her palm. Stroking it with slow up and down movements, she said, "I want you inside me. Now."

Tair choked out, "Kate…" and tried desperately to think.

Kate said, "I don't care. You win. We'll live on Shimeria. I don't care about anything except feeling you inside me." She gave him one last stroke and her hands went under her skirt to one of the ties of her panties. Tair's hand shot out, gripping her wrist, and stopping her.

Looking up at him in surprise, she tried to move her hand, but his grip was firm. He looked like he was in agony.

Tair cursed himself inwardly. He was insane. She was ready and willing. She trusted him. She had surrendered the game and agreed to live on Shimeria. All his careful building of trust and luring her closer had worked. She was vulnerable and greedy for him.

He had her right where he had planned. And he couldn't do it. The truth of it hit him squarely like a blow to the chest and rocked him all the way to his soul.

No matter how badly he wanted her, there was too much that she did not know and too many games between them. She was too vulnerable. He could no longer deny or pretend to himself or to her. The time for games without real meaning was over. Looking into her perplexed face, he said firmly, "No, Kate, not like this."

Kate was shocked not only at the words but the tone. He really meant it. He was rejecting her completely. She jerked her hand from his grasp with one fierce move and scrambled off of his lap.

Standing and staring at him, she watched as he grimaced and re-buttoned his pants. She said coldly, "What the hell kind of game are we playing now?"

Then, she added sarcastically, "Oh, yes, I remember this one. It's called make a fool out of Kate."

Tair rubbed a hand over his face. There was no going back. He could only go forward and fight for her. His heart raced and he felt terror run through him at the risk.

Finally, he took a deep breath and said calmly, "It is not a game, Kate, and that is the problem. You have been through too much today and you are vulnerable. I will not have our first time together overshadowed by other things. We need to reach an understanding first."

Kate felt frustrated arousal and fury blending to a lethal mix inside her. With icy composure, she said, "Why should you care? What possible difference does it make?"

Tair smiled at her grimly. He said simply, "It makes every difference. I am in love with you, Kate. No more games and hidden plots. I have fought it and denied it, and pretended it would go away. The truth is I will never stop loving you."

Kate felt pure panic all the way to her toes. In a shocked voice, she said, "Don't be ridiculous. You don't love me."

Tair gave a self-derisive laugh. "Kate, I am crazy with love for you. The only reason you cannot see it clearly, is because you love me, too."

She took a step back. Her whole world was upside down today and she couldn't seem to figure out which way was up. She grabbed for outward icy composure in the midst of such inner turmoil. "Now that really pisses me off. I never said that. You're crazy."

He laughed once again rather resignedly. "I admitted it already. And you do not have to say it. You tell me every day in a hundred small ways. The way your eyes light when you see me, the way you respond to my touch. The way you trust me, when you have every reason to distrust. You love me, Kate. And when you stop running from it, you will admit it."

Kate shook her head. He did not love her. She did not love him. It was a simple sexual affair and a game and this was getting out of hand. This overwhelming panic she felt was not good. She needed to think.

She needed to get away from him and think. She turned and headed for the bathroom, calling over her shoulder, "Wait right there, psycho, I'm just cleaning up."

He gave her a skeptical look, but nodded.

* * * * *

Kate shut the door of the bathroom and went to the mirror over the sink. Staring at the face in the mirror, she wondered what the hell had happened to Kate Carson. The woman staring back at her was a mess. Her face was red and blotchy from crying. Her hair was tangled and her eyes looked swollen.

She was pale and there was an overall look of tension and panic on her face. Grimacing, she muttered, "You're powerful, and confident, and you don't need anyone." The words echoed in the room as if mocking her.

She decided to handle one thing at a time. First of all, she would fix herself. Then she'd handle Tair.

Chapter 18

Tair waited impatiently for Kate to return. She would be more difficult now, he felt sure of it. She was panicked and when Kate was scared, she grew fierce. When she walked back into the room freshly groomed and with the light of battle in her eyes, he smiled grimly. And waited.

Kate felt much better. Her heart was thumping like she had run a race, but she was dealing with it. She needed to interject a little reality into this sentimental delusion of Tair's.

She squared her shoulders. "Tair, it has been a stressful day. Obviously, this has been more difficult for you than I thought."

Staring at him sternly, she said firmly, "I know I'm to blame with my emotional whig-out, but there's no reason for us to pretend things are anything but what they are. We are having a purely sexual affair due to this Oath business. I don't need love words and all that sentimental drivel."

Tair roared with laughter. She was priceless. He shook his head, marveling at her ability to blind herself to what she did not want to see.

Regaining control, he said calmly and emphatically, "I have never met anyone who needs sentimental drivel more than you, Kate."

Kate felt her heart rate climb, but she wasn't sure if it was temper or more panic. In an overly patient tone, she said, "You are not in touch with reality and need to seek help."

Tair grinned. "*Sheka*, you are the biggest fraud on two worlds. That is the reality."

Kate nearly smiled at his tone, but managed to keep her glare. She said coolly, "I am not a fraud. I don't know what you mean by that."

Tair eyed her with open amusement. "You show the world what a hard, dangerous person you are. You disdain anything that will make people think you are soft, or that you need anyone."

He swept his hand through the air, mimicking pulling back a curtain. He reeled off the list like a lawyer in court presenting evidence, gently mocking her. "Meanwhile, you sneak food to Deva and cuddle her when you think I do not know it. Your eyes grow wet at pledge ceremonies, and you are unbearably touched when I give you the simplest of sincere compliments."

He leaned forward and looked her squarely in the eyes, as he made the final point. "The slightest tenderness from me, and you are completely undone. That is evidence even a lawyer cannot deny."

Kate felt a sudden confusion. In defense, she attacked. "Maybe you do love me, but maybe that was part of my plan."

She searched desperately for the words to distance him. "I've been keeping you under control using your emotions. Then, I walk away the winner after two weeks. Have you considered that? I may be soft sometimes, but I'm pure bitch when it counts."

The smile drained from his face. He said quietly, "I believe you have proven your own words, *sheka*."

Kate felt regret slice through her. Her words had hurt him. She felt her own heart ache in response. She admitted softly, "I'm sorry. There was no plan."

He nodded solemnly. "I know."

Suddenly tired, Kate tried to think of a way to reason with him. She could barely focus. The exhaustion of the day and her emotional storm was catching up with her.

At this point, she was through pretending and plotting. "I need to think and I can't seem to do it. There's a spare bedroom. I would appreciate it if you would use it. I need to be away from you for tonight. I need some time alone."

Tair studied her in silence for a moment. Finally, he agreed. "You are tired, Kate. We will talk again after you have slept. It has been a very long, difficult day."

She gave him a look of gratitude. Her exhaustion ran bone deep. She was shaky and vulnerable, and her emotions were running too high for her to be able to think rationally. She would figure it all out in the morning. "Thank you."

He nodded. She walked to the hallway and looked back.

Tair smiled at her and said firmly, "I will be here in the morning, Kate. I will always be here to love you and fight with you. When you finally trust in that, you will find the rest is rather simple."

Kate gave him a look so tired and defeated that he ached to take her into his arms. Then she turned and walked down the hallway. Tair leaned back and ran his hands over his face. He was exhausted, too.

Love was no easy emotion, and loving Kate was an even more complicated thing. The very traits he loved about her, her strength, her prickly shields and wit, her hidden softness and inner passion, were the same things that made a love relationship difficult with her. He reached down and pulled off his boots.

The wait would be unbearable, but there was nothing he could do. He knew her better than she knew herself. She needed this time, so he would give it to her. But if she woke up tomorrow with the wrong answers, he was not giving up.

She needed him. They needed each other. Shaking his head at the two of them, he muttered, "She issues a sexual challenge and I raise the stakes with an emotional one. I don't know which of us is the bigger fool."

Chapter 19

Kate thought about Tair's words as she tossed and turned in bed that night. Despite her exhaustion, she could not sleep. His words kept echoing in her head. Sometimes the truth is too powerful to deny. She had avoided it her whole life, but now it was staring her in the face.

She was afraid to love anyone fully because the risk was so great. She loved Gage and Sharon, but it was the inescapable love formed by siblings. Sharon hadn't been born her sister, but she had known Sharon since she was eight.

She loved them both with the kind of love that comes in spite of reason or choice. It had taken root over time and grown too deeply to ever be cut out. It was simply a fact.

Her feelings for Tair were more complicated and scary. She was scared spitless at the thought of loving him. She had avoided emotion in her past relationships, quickly cutting off contact at the first stirrings of anything beyond respect and affection. At other times, she drove the person away, like she had with Todd. With new clarity, she realized it was a protection from loss. She turned onto her side.

If she loved Tair, he could abandon her. And the longer they were together, and the more her love grew, the greater that final loss. It was an incredible and awful risk.

With painful honesty, she admitted what she had known for some time. She was already in love with him. He was sexy and funny. She admired his integrity and his intelligence. She might not agree with him all the time, but she believed in him. He was a good man.

The most amazing thing was his ability to see her – not the outer Kate, but the inner Kate. He was psychic and that accounted for a lot of it. But, she had a gut feeling that even if he had no ability to read her mind, he would have seen her. And still loved her.

The real choice was whether to stay with him and risk losing him later, or to cut her losses and deal with the pain now. Just the thought of a life without Tair left her feeling cold and empty inside.

Turning over onto her back, she stared into the darkness. Why was she so convinced it wouldn't work? Would Tair really just throw up his hands and give up on the two of them at some point? Would she?

That didn't sound like Tair at all. He was one of the most determined men she had ever encountered. He was very strong-willed and not one to back away when things grew rough. He was a fighter.

With a sudden smile, she realized he was also one of the smartest people she had ever met. Maybe she needed to look at this whole thing from another view.

Turning over onto her side, she hugged her pillow and considered. It boiled down to gambling and guts in the end. Did she trust him and herself enough to take the risk of getting hurt? Did she have the guts to take the chance? Did she want it enough? Did she want *him* enough?

Did she love him enough to take the chance? Her breath caught. The answer came in the simplest of ways -- an undeniable voice from deep inside her soul.

Yes. If she was going to gamble it all, it was going to be with Tair. And if anything was worth fighting for, it was their love. In her short time with Tair, she had discovered a happiness that she was not willing to lose.

For the first time in her life, she was happier with someone than alone. She was going to fight to keep it. She would bet on the two of them.

She was Kate Carson, newly honest, mostly confident, pretty powerful, and genuine hell-on-wheels. And she was insanely in love with a sexy psychic alien cop who felt the same way about her. She fought the impulse to laugh with the sheer joy of it.

Really, it *was* simple. Tair had cut through to the heart of it. Her eyes grew heavy as she relaxed, finally. Her last thought was of Tair as she drifted into sleep. She had big plans for him. He was in for a surprise. There was the small matter of a declaration of love to make. Then, she had a Challenge to settle.

Chapter 20

The next morning, Kate awakened slowly. Reaching out with one hand, she searched for the warmth of Tair's body. He was not in bed.

As she opened her eyes, the events of the previous day flashed through her mind. Torn between nerves and elation, she wondered what to say to Tair. She realized he was still blocking her at the same time that the emptiness of the apartment registered. He was not here. She felt sure of it.

Climbing out of bed, she wandered into the living room and found a note on the table by the couch. She studied the large masculine scrawl for a moment. His handwriting was atrocious. He should have been a health engineer, not a cop. She smiled.

Kate Harmony Carson —

By my authority as Guardian, you are under arrest for theft. The punishment for stealing a heart is a lifetime sentence.

It is time for our final Challenge. The first one to say the word "please" forfeits. You many resist, but prepare to lose.

You will say it, sheka, and then you will tell me what we both know. I will return soon. I will return always.

-- Tair

Kate shook her head. Only Tair could manage to melt her heart, infuriate her with his smugness, and challenge her competitive instincts all at the same time. She laughed. There was no one like him. She stood there grinning.

She thought about it for a moment. She needed a shower and the proper combat attire. Grimacing, she thought about how she looked currently. At the moment she had bed hair. No way was she playing the most important game of her life looking like Medusa on a bad hair day.

With determined, purposeful strides she headed to the bathroom. She knew exactly the outfit to bring Tair to his knees. Inwardly smiling with satisfaction, she felt a thrill of anticipation run through her.

She would tell him she loved him. She would pledge with him and move to Shimeria, too. It was a big step, but she was willing to take it. Shimeria might be male-dominated and very different from her own planet, but she would carve her own path there.

They would find a way to combine their two cultures. She was up to the challenge of creating a new life. She knew what she wanted and she planned to get it. However, first she was going to teach Tair that Kate Carson played to win. Always.

Chapter 21

Kate heard the slam of the front door and checked the mirror one last time. With a smile, she stared at her reflection. The woman was Kate, but the image was pure sex.

Her hair cascaded down into artfully arranged waves. She looked sexily mussed. It had taken nearly forty minutes of preparation to look that carefully disarrayed.

She had on just a trace of light makeup to give her some confidence, but to look natural. She smoothed the red silk teddy. It hugged her breasts and hips emphasizing her curves. She wore nothing under it.

Being three snaps away from totally nude made her blood heat a little. Tair was going to be in for a fight. She had taken the time to slather on her favorite cream, so her body under the teddy was soft and smooth. It would drive him crazy. Basically, she was hitting him with the full arsenal from the very beginning. She knew she looked her best.

She studied the mirror with satisfaction. She was no beauty queen, but she knew how to work with the material at hand. In her dealings with males, she had learned a secret. Sex appeal was more about confidence than perfection. It was about enjoying your body and letting that enjoyment show.

Running her hands over her breasts, she watched as her nipples tightened in response. She was ready to enjoy. She was ready to take on Tair.

Feeling her heart rate speed up, she turned just as he entered the bedroom. They both froze, inhaling with surprise.

Tair stopped dead in the doorway, his mind going blank as powerful arousal struck him squarely. Kate was breathtaking. She looked like she had stepped out of one of *his* fantasies.

Her hair was streaming down over her shoulders. The tiny garment barely covered the curves of her body, more of a seductive tease than anything. He felt his blood surge as his cock went rock hard in an instant.

He clenched his hands and fought the urge to take her immediately. The need rose inside him and he struggled for calm. He had expected her to be prepared, but not this prepared.

Suppressing his raging desire, he reached for the iron control that others so often admired. It was not easy, but eventually he was able to get his breathing under control and his brain functioning. He searched her face, shocked anew by the visible love in her eyes.

Kate had found the right answers. His relief was tremendous. Joy and elation fought equally in his chest. He thought about unblocking and scanning her, but decided against it. He wasn't sure his control would last if he joined with her now or knew the thoughts running through her mind.

Kate had undergone her own struggle for control. When he appeared in the doorway, she was struck by a sense of rightness so great she trembled with it. She had not realized, in all her seductive plotting, what it would feel like to see him now-- knowing and admitting that she loved him.

This big, incredible man belonged to her. Despite being on different planets, despite everything, he had found her. And he loved her. The sheer wonder of it overwhelmed her.

It was not that he looked any different. He had on his Guardian black shirt and black pants, with newly shined boots. What caught and held her attention, though, was the expression on his face when he saw her.

He looked at her as if she was the answer to every question he'd ever had. He looked at her like the world began and ended with her. And he looked at her with a desire so powerful that it bordered on violent.

Her knees went weak in anticipation. For a moment she had been certain he would walk straight to her and unleash the desire driving him. Her mouth went dry and her sex grew wet as she watched him struggle for control. Finally, he seemed to leash his storm of emotion.

He leaned against the doorway. He stared right into her eyes. His voice was husky but utterly sincere. "Never in my lifetime will I forget how beautiful you look at this moment."

Kate felt her smile widen. "You know what you do to me when you say stuff like that."

She saw his gaze drift downward again. She tried to focus. The Challenge. His note. "Nice note, by the way. I think it's time I introduce you to the concept of humility. But don't worry. It won't hurt. Much." She laughed.

Tair grinned. She was a fighter. "Ahh, *sheka*, I must disagree. I think it is time to introduce you to the pleasures of losing."

He let his gaze roam over her body and watched the flush rise in her face. "Ahhh. Our Challenge. At last. I am eager to begin. Do you know what most of your fantasies have in common, Kate?"

Kate felt the heat rising and strove for a normal, rather disinterested tone. "I'm sure you feel compelled to tell me."

He didn't smile. Instead, his eyes grew darker. He spoke in that softer, tempting voice that he used so effectively. "You dream of a man who will overwhelm you. You lie awake, in the dark, touching yourself and yearning for a lover who will push you past control, past reason, past limits."

He straightened from the doorway. "He would have to be someone as strong as you are, or stronger. Someone you respect and trust. Someone you love enough to allow beyond all of your barriers and defenses."

Kate slid her eyes away from his as the truth of it struck her. He was right, of course. She was incredibly aroused by and somewhat scared of the idea at the same time. It was the thrill of it. The real challenge. She yearned to truly let go with someone and really trust.

Tair's ordered in a hard voice. "Look at me, Kate."

Kate brought her eyes back to his. He reached for the top button of his shirt. "Never doubt, I am that man."

He unbuttoned his shirt slowly, watching her face. The look in his eyes was intent. She had his full attention. As she watched his deliberate movements, something inside her quaked. At last he reached the last button. "Sit on the bed."

Kate arched an eyebrow and felt a little spurt of defiance at the tone. "Why?"

He smiled. "Compliance, Kate. You are still under Oath. You will be doing a lot of complying in this bedroom today. I assume you do not wish to argue each time. When one chooses to play, one plays by the rules. You are meeting my Challenge."

He dared her. "Or am I wrong?"

Kate shot him a hard look, but moved over and sat down on the bed. "Will this do, Mr. I'm-Such-A-Masterful-Hardass?"

Tair laughed. "For now. And, *sheka*, you might re-consider that attitude. I am in the position of power at the moment."

Kate smiled, running her eyes over his body. The shirt was open and she could see parts of his chest. He looked delicious. Those pants were noticeably tight in the crotch. Oh yes, he was feeling the pressure, too.

She reached up and cupped one of her breasts. Thumbing the nipple, she enjoyed herself for a moment, all the while watching his face. His eyes followed her hand. "Are you?"

Tair's gaze shot to her face. "Yes, I am."

Shrugging out of the shirt, he tossed it onto a nearby chair. Then, apparently changing his mind, he walked over to the chair picked up the shirt. He sat down and tossed the shirt to the floor.

Kate watched the muscles rippling in his chest with appreciation. He was so sexy wearing just those pants and boots. Very darkly dangerous and erotic.

She felt her mouth water. He was watching her with such focused intensity. It might have been a little intimidating, but she was aroused nonetheless. Besides, no one intimidated her. She was Kate Carson, after all.

He smiled slowly. "Since you have begun, I think you should continue, *sheka*. Use both hands. I want those nipples hard and very sensitive when I take them into my mouth."

Kate shuddered a little at the words. She had paused in her teasing while he walked to the chair. Now, reaching up, she cupped her other breast and began toying with both nipples through the delicate fabric. It felt wonderful, but she ached for his mouth. She started to close her eyes instinctively and then struggled to keep them open.

Tair watched her. He reached for the top button of his pants, then leaned down instead and pulled off each boot. "Keep your eyes open. And spread your legs."

Kate sat back on the bed a little and moved each leg until she was facing him, open and vulnerable. She was extremely conscious of the small swatch of fabric with those three snaps separating her from his gaze. She knew the fabric was wet already.

Tair gave her an approving nod. Leaning back in the chair, he reached for the button on his pants and paused. "Use you right hand and touch your clit. Play with it, *sheka*. You know what feels good. But keep your gaze on me."

Kate nodded. She was feeling the heat now. She didn't mind a few suggestions. Bringing her hand down, she ran it over the fabric of the teddy and over her mound. Reaching her clit, she touched herself lightly. Pleasure ran through her at the teasing sensation. She nearly moaned.

Tair unbuttoned his pants and then spread the material apart. His hard cock sprang free. He looked huge and hard and ready. She swallowed. He took one hand and ran it down the length of the shaft. She tore her eyes from his cock and looked at his face. It reflected unself-conscious pleasure.

He gave her a sexy half-smile. "Do you like what you see?"

She smiled, then moaned a little when he took his cock in his hand and stroked slowly up and down, watching her. "Yes."

His smile widened, although his eyes shifted to her sex. "Can you imagine how it will feel when I fill you, Kate? Are you ready for me yet? We will not stop this time."

Kate nodded eagerly. She was soaking wet. All those times of stopping just short of intercourse ran through her head. It would be different this time. She would feel his hard cock pumping inside her.

He said softly, "You want it. You need only say one small word. Say it, Kate."

Kate felt the shock of his statement hit her. She was getting caught up and losing control. She focused. "No."

He stopped the motion of his hand and laughed, although it was strained. "I did not think you would surrender so easily, but I was giving you the choice. Remember you had the chance, *sheka*."

He stood up. He pulled his pants down over his hips and then stepped out of them, kicking them out of his way. Striding over to the bed, he said, "On your back. Now."

She shivered. He looked so aggressive standing there in front of her. With a little start of surprise, she realized this was a side of Tair that she had not fully seen. Even without her compliance oath, she realized he could physically over-power her.

There was just enough doubt to be aroused and yet still feel safe. He would never hurt her no matter the provocation. Still, the sense of danger was strangely thrilling and intoxicating to her.

She scooted back on the bed slowly. He stood there watching her. She was about to lean back when he said, "Wait. Are you fond of this garment?"

She froze, confused. "Fond of it? Well, I have another one in black."

He grinned. "I look forward to it."

Climbing on the bed, he crawled until he sat next to her. He reached up and ran his hand along her cheek in a tender gesture. She was caught off guard at the touch.

Would he settle on one mood, for goodness sake? He was making her crazy. She narrowed her eyes. Maybe that was the point. She felt off-balance, unsure what would happen next. Was he going to rip the teddy off?

He reached out with the other hand and stroked her gently along the top of her shoulder. She felt the strap of her teddy moving along with his hand. He moved it downward until it was off her shoulder and hanging loosely on her arm. Moving his other hand from her face, he stroked her neck. Eventually, the strap on that shoulder met the same fate.

She felt her breath catch as the material of the teddy fell downward a little, clinging to the tops of her breasts. He looked into her eyes and said, "Don't move."

She saw his head move downward and felt him kiss along her neck. He paused occasionally and sucked, then moved further down. She fought to keep still, aching to feel his mouth on her tight nipples.

He kept moving downward until he was kissing the upper swells of her breasts right above the fabric. She arched a little instinctively. He pulled back and shot her a hard look. "I will not say it again."

She froze. He leaned down and kissed his way along the fabric, until she was ready to scream in frustration. Finally, he darted his tongue along the edge, narrowly missing her nipple.

She moaned and fought to stay still. This was slow, sensual torture. He knew how sensitive her nipples were and how much she loved his mouth there. He was prolonging her anticipation, and it was working.

She heard him mutter against the top of the fabric. "If your nipples are not hard enough, we will start over again from the beginning."

He eased his head away, and looked at her. He reached one hand and pulled the teddy downward, baring her breast. With the other hand, he bared the other breast. She inhaled and waited.

He said softly, "You are so beautiful."

The cool air of the room tightened her nipples even more under his gaze. She bit her lip. Finally, he leaned forward and licked around one hard nipple, carefully avoiding it. She moaned, feeling like grabbing his head and forcing him to take it into his mouth. At the sound he swirled his tongue around the hard tip, as if in reward.

She felt the wet slide of his tongue and trembled. It felt so good. Now if he would only suck on it. She had no sooner thought it than he complied. He opened his mouth and drew her nipple into it, sucking with gentle pressure. As she felt his moist heat sucking on her, she moaned louder.

He released her nipple and then used his tongue to toy with her again. It was maddening, delicious torment. She could feel herself losing focus. He switched to the other breast, subjecting it to the same treatment. He used his hand to gently tug and toy with her other nipple.

Finally, Kate gave up and arched into his mouth. She brought both hands up and grabbed the back of his head. Running her hands through his dark hair, she trembled and said, "Oh, that feels so good...so good..."

He licked around her nipple with gentle skill. Kate heard his voice as if from a distance. "Say it, Kate, and I will make you feel even better."

She cursed inwardly. Of course. The Challenge. She struggled to find some semblance of control. Her voice when it emerged sounded angry. "No."

His head came up with a snap. He stared at her a moment. Then he reached downward abruptly and cupped her sex. She was shocked at the swiftness of the move. As he fondled her gently, she closed her eyes.

He said, "On your back now, *sheka*."

She leaned back until she felt the soft bed under her. Spreading her legs a little, she arched up into his hand. He was giving her just enough pressure to feel good, but not enough. She needed more.

He said, "Wider."

She spread her legs further apart. In response he pressed the heel of his palm harder against her mound, right over her clit. Pleasure radiated outward from the spot. She groaned.

He pulled his hand away. She opened her eyes in surprise and protest. She wanted more. He moved over her until he was between her legs, half sitting. He said softly, "Close your eyes, Kate."

She closed her eyes and waited. Finally, she felt his mouth on her mound through the thin fabric. As he licked and sucked her, she moaned and reached for his head. She felt him pull away in response as he ordered, "Hands by your head, *sheka*. I am the one in control here."

Kate moved her hands slowly until they rested beside her head. She was past protesting. At this point, she wanted more of his mouth. If she needed to follow a few directions to get it, she would do it. No problem. She felt the hot swirl of his tongue through the fabric against her clit and trembled. He played with her for endless moments, and her arousal rose with each delicate lick.

Finally, she felt his hand tease along the edge of the teddy. She held her breath, waiting. He jerked and the snaps gave way. She opened her eyes in surprise and then shut them again quickly. She felt him lean over her again. He grabbed the teddy with both hands and ripped it apart like paper, leaving her completely bare.

Kate's heart was racing and she was breathing hard. She kept her eyes closed even as she felt one finger play along her opening. She was so wet. She raised her hips, eager for more of his touch.

He moved upward teasing her clit. At that moment, she realized something that should have occurred to her long before now. He knew her, inside and out. He knew from previous lovemaking just what touches she liked and what really made her scream.

He knew mentally just what she liked as well. He knew how to push and when to back off. This game was one that she might lose. She felt the probe of one long finger into her sex.

Tair said softly, "I am going to scan you now, Kate. I will know exactly what you are thinking. I will know when you want more and what you want next. And I am going to push you harder than you ever dreamed you could be pushed."

He stroked his finger slowly in and out of her. "And then you are going to surrender. You will say the word, but the word is meaningless really. You are going to give in to me, because it is what you want."

He leaned down and hovered over her mound. She could feel his breath as he spoke. "It is what I want, too. Trust me, Kate, and let go."

She felt his tongue lick around her clit and whimpered. He kept the movements of his finger slow as he teased and tormented her. He licked and sucked as she moaned. She shook her head no. She was not giving in.

He said against her sex, "Yes, Kate. You will."

He added another finger and stroked her faster. She could feel him pressing upward with each movement, hitting the upper wall of her sex with just enough pressure. He licked and stroked her until she wanted to scream at the pleasurable torment of it. She felt out of control and close to the edge of release. Just a little more.

He withdrew his fingers and mouth suddenly. Before she could help it, she said, "Don't stop."

He moved upward and then rested his weight on his elbows. She felt the hard length of his cock against her mound and shuddered under him. He was making her crazy. She muttered, "You know what I want. Give it to me."

He moved down a little until the head of his cock was probing her opening. She gave a relieved moan and arched upward to accommodate him. He moved abruptly and pinned her hips with his, but he did not press into her. He ordered, "Open your eyes, Kate."

Kate opened her eyes. He was looming over her, his eyes staring into hers. They were dark with arousal and his face was nakedly hungry. He leaned down and placed a gentle kiss on her mouth. Rising back up, he said softly, "I want you. I need you. I love you."

Kate shook at his words. She swallowed hard, but her mind was completely blank. She felt the hard pressure of him between her legs. His eyes were staring at her with desire and love. She whimpered and whispered, "I can't...Tair...please..."

At that last word, he leaned down again and kissed her hard on the mouth. Then his cock plunged into her. She felt the hard pressure sliding into her aching sex and cried out. He was huge and it was too much. She tightened up without really meaning to do it.

He moaned and gritted out, "Relax, Kate. Please. You can take me."

She gasped and struggled to relax her tense body. She felt him pull back a little inside her and then slide gently forward. He went a little further. Kate relaxed as a surge of pleasure went through her.

With the next stroke, he filled her completely. He paused, obviously giving her time to adjust to his intrusion. She shut her eyes at the intensity of the feeling, savoring it. Then she opened her eyes and smiled. "I didn't think you were going to fit there for a minute."

He smiled back at her, although the smile turned into a grimace toward the end. He pulled back from her and muttered, "I will."

He drove into her and arched his spine. Kate let out a small scream in surprise and pleasure. It felt fantastic. He stroked out of her and then surged forward filling her again. On the inward stroke, he thrust into her mind.

Kate felt his desire and pleasure flood her and let out another scream, this one a little louder. Then she moaned and arched her hips upward, eager to meet his thrusts.

He swore and said, "That's it. You are mine now. Mine!"

Kate moaned and grabbed his hips, digging her fingernails into his ass. He groaned. The slap of their bodies was loud in the silence of the room. Pleasure built between the two of them as Tair shared his and she shared hers. Kate was blind, deaf, and out of control. She clawed at him, wanting more.

Tair plunged into her with greater strength and speed. Finally, she hung on the edge of release and her body tensed. He muttered, "Now. Kate. Now."

Kate screamed as wave after wave of pleasure ran through her. She was lost in it, beyond all thought. She could only feel. She heard Tair moan loudly and felt the liquid warmth of him flood inside her as his own release hit her. It was too much

She felt her breath catch and her vision grayed. She shut her eyes and rode the pleasure until it began to recede. Then, she took in great gulps of air.

Tair collapsed on her, and then rolled to her side. He was breathing harshly, obviously trying to catch his breath, too. Finally, they calmed. Kate began to think about what had just happened. She frowned a little, but couldn't seem to find the energy to get truly angry. She turned her head, and found him watching her. She arched an eyebrow and said simply, "Congratulations. Although somehow I don't feel like much of a loser."

He merely smiled. She thought about it for a moment and then finally admitted, "You know, if you had pushed me that hard from the beginning I might have caved then. I don't know."

Tair chuckled. "No, you would not have surrendered in the beginning. You only surrendered now because of your feelings for me. And only because it was what you wanted."

He placed a gentle hand on her forehead and smoothed back her hair. "You are quite a fighter, *sheka*. It is one of the things I love about you."

Kate swallowed hard. Here it was. That moment. She had never said it before to a lover. She fought a sudden bad attack of nerves.

Tair's eyes held a wealth of understanding. His hand traced the curve of her face. He said softly, "I know how hard it is to say it, *sheka*. I have lost loved ones, too. My parents died. I lost a friend once in my work. It is a great risk."

His hand paused. His voice was still soft despite the intensity of his words. "The biggest risk. It is why I fought so hard to keep from loving you. I denied it, and pretended, and even waited, hoping it would pass. We are the same underneath, you and I."

Kate gave him a shaky smile. Her heart was racing again. She took a deep breath and then choked out, "I..lo..loveyoutoo."

Tair laughed as elation flooded him. She had said it. True, she had nearly choked on the words, but she had said it. She had admitted it.

He threw back his head and then laughed again. Finally, he placed a hard kiss on her mouth. Leaning back away from her, he grinned. "We will practice saying it, *sheka*. Why, when we have been pledged for many years, you may even be as good as I am at saying it."

She narrowed her eyes at him. "Very funny."

She felt his happiness and relief wash through her. She felt his love surround her, almost a tangible thing. She smiled. "I love you, Tair. Really. No games, no plots, and no hidden agendas. I love you."

He looked surprised and even touched at her sudden words. "Thank you, Kate."

He frowned a little. "You realize there are no real losers in this bed, regardless of the games that are played. Do you not?"

She laughed. "Oh yeah. I figured that out."

The she leaned forward and kissed him softly. His mouth moved under hers in response and increasing interest. Finally, she rose and looked down at him. With a big grin, she asked, "Now, how 'bout we go best two out of three?"

Chapter 22

Kate stood outside the health building. The night air was cool, but she was enjoying it. She and Tair had spent hours with Gage in his health center room. She had been kicked out so that the two men could talk privately. She laughed, trying to imagine that conversation.

She started walking along the path that led around the health building grounds, enjoying the air and the quiet of the night. Tair and Gage were arrogant and annoying alike in some ways. They would either become friends or kill each other.

Of course, they had one really big thing in common. They both loved her. With the thought, she laughed again, this time with pure joy. It was a beautiful night.

Gage was going to be fine. She and Tair had begun making plans to start their life together. They had a lot to figure out, but they would do it. Well, if they could stay out of bed long enough to do anything.

They had spent the day all over each other. They had called the health center every few hours until she was given permission to visit Gage again. He was doing a lot better today. For once, everything felt right. She felt on top of the world. Nothing could stop her now.

Hearing a rustle from behind her, she stopped and announced in frigid tones, "If you're a mugger, you're in trouble. I've had one hellava time lately. I'll kill you simply for the emotional release. If you're Jadik, quit slinking around back there, you stalker." She spun around and put her hands on her hips.

Jadik stepped into the light and said indignantly, "I do not *slink*. I was watching over you. I do not *stalk* either."

Kate laughed, amused by his affronted male pride. Walking forward, she placed a brief, hard kiss on his mouth, and said, "Hello, Jadik. I'm headed back toward the health center. No need to get me angry by being overprotective. You're welcome to walk back with me if you like."

Jadik grinned at her. He studied her radiant face for a moment, deducing the reason behind it. As the two of them began walking, he said with genuine pleasure, "You have figured it out."

Kate shot him a quizzical look and asked, "Figured what out?"

He said, "You and Tair are in love with each other. It is obvious to all."

Rolling her eyes, she complained, "Nothing like being the last one to know."

They laughed and continued walking in companionable silence until Kate said with concern, "You know, Jadik, you seem to be walking with a slight limp. Are you okay?"

Jadik grimaced. "Yes, I am fine. It was nothing."

Hearing the male defensiveness in his voice, Kate wondered at the cause. "How did it happen?"

He paused and looked down at her concerned face. Shaking his head at his own foolish pride, he said, "I have found my pactmate. I spoke with her yesterday."

Kate was surprised and pleased. "What happened?"

Jadik smiled at her excitement. "I have the ability to show you what happened. It will feel like a memory for you. One of my more useful abilities. With your permission, I will show you." When she nodded, he focused and replayed the entire incident for Kate.

Kate saw what happened like a memory in her mind. At the end, she threw back her head and laughed. She couldn't help it. "She knocked you on your ass."

He shot her a glare. "My thanks for your sympathy."

Kate was trying to control her laughter, but it wasn't easy. "And she's such a little thing, too."

Jadik gave her a lethal look. She said solemnly, "But mean. She's very mean."

He rolled his eyes at her and she laughed once again. She grabbed his arm and said, "Come on, tough guy, you'll have to walk it off." They walked companionably, joking and enjoying each other's company.

Finally, they reached the outside door of the building. Kate stopped and turned when she realized Jadik was not coming in with her. She studied him a moment.

He looked so alone, standing there in the dark. She took a step toward him. "Jadik, I know you're leaving, and I won't insist you come up with me.

But I'd like you know something important. I wish you well. I want you to be happy. I want you to find the kind of happiness I feel with Tair."

He smiled his beautiful angel smile at her and said simply, "Thank you, Kate."

Something was nagging at her. It had to do with him, too. A chance remark Tair had made at one time...something about Jadik being able to find anyone.

Jadik turned to go, but then stopped when Kate called out quickly, "Oh, Jadik, wait! I meant to ask. How did you find me? I didn't tell anyone I was going for a walk. It was an impulse."

He turned around slowly and flashed her a smug smile. His next words were heavy with emphasis. "I am a Tracker. Finding people is my profession."

His words registered and then several things clicked into place. Kate winced as she thought of his running pactmate. "Uh oh. Does Cass know that?"

Unholy amusement shone from Jadik's face. "If she does not know it now, she will know it very soon." He winked at her and walked off, blending into the dark night.

Kate opened the door and spotted Tair coming toward her. She smiled at him and walked into his arms, but her curiosity was killing her. Raising her head, she asked, "Just how good a tracker is Jadik?"

Tair looked confused for a moment and then he laughed. "He is the best tracker I have ever known. He is relentless. I would not want to attempt to escape him."

Kate shook her head. "Somehow I knew you were going to say that."

Shimerian Series

1. Oath of Seduction: Seducing Sharon (anthology *The Best Of Ellora's Cave: Volume I*)
2. Oath Of Challenge: Conquering Kate
3. Oath Of Capture: Capturing Cass

About the author:

Critically acclaimed Marly Chance is an Ellora's Cave best-selling author. Her first title, *Oath of Seduction: Seducing Sharon*, was selected as a top pick in women's erotica by Romantic Times magazine. A full-time writer, Marly lives in a small town in Tennessee with her husband.

She welcomes gifts of chocolate and mail from readers! You can visit her on the web at www.marlychance.com or write to her c/o Ellora's Cave Publishing at P.O. Box 787, Hudson, Ohio 44236-0787.